Charles Allen

Levels of Pennsylvania

Charles Allen

Levels of Pennsylvania

ISBN/EAN: 9783337427788

Printed in Europe, USA, Canada, Australia, Japan

Cover: Foto ©Andreas Hilbeck / pixelio.de

More available books at **www.hansebooks.com**

SECOND
GEOLOGICAL SURVEY OF PENNSYLVANIA

J. P. LESLEY, STATE GEOLOGIST.

1008 Clinton Street, Philada., May 11, 1876.

SIR:

By order of the Board of Commissioners of the Geological Survey, I detailed Mr. Charles Allen, of Harrisburg, to the special work of collecting and collating the Levels of the State, for the use of the Geological Corps, Railway Engineers, County Surveyors, and other citizens.

Mr. Allen's preliminary tables were considered by the American Philosophical Society to be of sufficient scientific value to publish in their Proceedings at the expense of the Society.

Three hundred extra copies were struck off for the use of the Survey, which I have instructed Mr. Allen to distribute by mail to those who furnished him with data, and to others who may be likely to aid in correcting and enlarging the record.

Please find enclosed *two* (duplicate) copies mailed to your address; one, to be kept by you for present use, and *the other to receive your notes, corrections, additions, criticisms, explanations, or remarks, and to be mailed to the following address:*

MR. CHARLES ALLEN,

OFFICE OF THE SECOND GEOLOGICAL SURVEY,

223 MARKET STREET,

Harrisburg, Pa.

When all the duplicate copies are returned, and their notes discussed, the Levels of the field-parties of the Survey got during 1874, 1875, will be added, and the whole will then be published as one of the regular series of Reports of the Survey, with the title:

REPORT OF PROGRESS FOR 1876

LEVELS OF PENNSYLVANIA

BY CHARLES ALLEN.

I trust that you will feel a real pleasure in taking part in this important piece of State work, and give the subject your earliest and most careful attention.

With great respect, your obedient servant,

J. P. LESLEY.

Contributions to the Physical Geography of the United States, by Charles Allen, Assistant in charge of the Collection and Collation of Railroad and other Levels for the Second Geological Survey of Pennsylvania.

By J. P. Lesley.

(*Read before the American Philosophical Society, January* 15, 1876.)

In presenting to the attention of the members Mr. Allen's list of Pennsylvania levels, I have only to say that the progress of physical geography in the United States has been so rapid, of late years, as to attract the attention of the Scientific world at home and abroad, and that its connection with the progress of geological science is so intimate, that working geologists hail with lively pleasure the publication of all hypsometrical records of a genuine kind, whether old or new. For want of government bureaus of statistics the greater part of such records have been irrecoverably lost. Of the tentative work of our railway, canal, slackwater and turnpike companies, done between 1830 and 1860, scarcely a trace remains; although, if its records could be recovered and printed, they would furnish copy for hundreds of volumes. Since 1860 the destruction has not been so complete, but has been nevertheless very great. There are recent important surveys of which no records can be found, even in the offices of the companies for whom they were made.

This important subject has received well-deserved attention at the hands of the chiefs of the United States Exploring Expeditions, who are mapping the interior of the Continent. But some efficient organization is required for the preservation and publication of levels in the States lying between the Atlantic and the Mississippi.

The State Geologists of Ohio and North Carolina, also, have published valuable hypsometric tables.

A beginning has now been made in Pennsylvania; and the following pages contain the records of the height above some assumed datum, reduced to tide level, of all stations on railways in the State, and in its immediate vicinity.

These records have mostly been obtained by personal examination of the profiles preserved at the offices; and in some cases, by letter, from superintendents and engineers. The greatest interest in the Collection has been manifested by members of the profession of Civil Engineering to whom application has been made; and in some instances, where records were wanting, new levelings have been ordered and the results transmitted.

Short headings are prefixed to the records, stating place, date and authority; and foot notes appended to them, stating difficulties of adjustment, incongruities, or doubts.

That a work of this nature should have the advantage of first publication in the transactions of the oldest Scientific Society of America, whose first President was Benjamin Franklin, and whose hall stands side by side with the ancient Capitol of the United States, is my reason for asking that this first systematic attempt on a large scale to render permanent and useful to all engineers and surveyors the scattered and perishable records of heights above sea-level of several thousand points in our valleys and on our mountains should be accepted by the Society.

It must be understood, however, that these lists require thorough re-examination and correction before they can be adopted as constants of science for the future. There are considerable difficulties yet to be encountered by such as undertake to harmonise the data of our railway surveys. Indeed, considering the imperfect way in which such surveys are necessarily made,—the accumulation of errors of instrumentation and personal equation along every long spirit-level line,—the uncertainty even of the tide-level datum at every head of tide,—the frequent lack of notes stating whether railway levels cross each other on grade, or not,—and the not uncommon fact that, after location-surveys have been made, the road-beds have been tempered up, or down, to suit convenience, and no record of the fact been kept, except in the memory of some division engineer no longer in the employ of the Company,—it is surprising that the errors of terminal or crossing adjustment are so few and small. But to render the record perfect all such errors, however few and small, must be eliminated; and this can only be accomplished by a zealous interest taken in the subject by resident engineers; who are therefore earnestly requested to co-operate to this end.

Geologists are dependent for the goodness of their field-work on accurate base-line levels. And it is to be hoped that a complete exhibition of the surface contour of Pennsylvania will sooner or later be obtained from a collation of the thousands of transit-lines and barometer-lines now in progress in all the districts occupied by the Assistant Geologists of the Survey. All their lines of levels are, however, based on the railroad records, and the publication of these in a corrected form is a necessary preliminary step.

If movements are still taking place in the crust of the earth,—and the frequent occurrence of slight earthquake shocks, in all the States of the Union, seems to speak in favor of the supposition,—physical philosophers are peculiarly interested in an early establishment of a universal hypsometrical record. From this point of view, also, it would seem especially germain to the origin and history of the American Philosophical Society to initiate such a record.

The net-work of Surveys which cover Pennsylvania may be divided into nine systems:

1. The Pennsylvania Central east and west system, from Trenton through Philadelphia, Harrisburg, Altoona, Pittsburgh, to Steubenville, and Youngstown, in Ohio; with numerous longer or shorter side branches.

2. The Reading Railroad northwest and southeast system, with many short branches in the Schuylkill Anthracite Field, and through the country in front of it between the Delaware and Susquehanna Rivers. It has been extended also to the

waters of the Upper Susquehanna, and will penetrate into New York State.

3. The North Pennsylvania north and south system, with numerous branches in the Lehigh and Wilkesbarre Anthracite Fields, in connection with the two Lehigh Valley Railroads, extending into the State of New York.

4. The Northern Central north and south system, extending from Baltimore, in Maryland, to Elmira, in New York, with several short branches.

5. The Philadelphia and Erie northwest system, with important branches crossing to the Alleghany River, and into the State of New York.

6. The Alleghany River north and south system, from Pittsburgh to the Oil Region, and Buffalo in New York.

7. The Baltimore and Ohio system, with its Connellsville branch to Pittsburgh, and its short coal and coke branch.

8. The Beaver River system, north and south, along the western margin of the State.

9. The Philadelphia, Wilmington and Baltimore southwest system.

The following tables are arranged in the above order, and will explain themselves:

I. The Pennsylvania R. R. System.

I. Pennsylvania Railroad.

Note.—The elevations at the various stations, on the Pennsylvania Railroad, were copied from the Engineers' notes, by permission of Mr. W. H. Wilson, its Consulting Engineer.

The datum, or base of levels, is ordinary high-water in Schuylkill River. This datum, according to Mr. James T. Gardener's determination, is 6.913 feet* above mean surface of the Atlantic Ocean. *These 7 feet are added in the second column.* Decimal parts of a foot do not occur in these lists. When below .5 they have been omitted; when more than .5 a whole number has been substituted.

*Permanent U. S. Coast Survey granite bench at Gloucester Ferry, N. J., opposite Philadelphia, is 8.10 above Mean Tide Raritan Bay, or Mean Ocean level. Mean Tide Delaware River = 8.10 — 4.751 = 3.349. Philadelphia City Surveyor's datum: 8.10 — 0.632 = 8.732. Pennsylvania R. R. Engineer's datum: 8.10 — 1.819 High tide, 6.913.

Pennsylvania R. R. Main Line.

STATIONS.	High Tide, Philad'a.	Above mean level Atlantic Ocean.
Philadelphia, Market Street........	25	32
West Philadelphia................	27	34
Powelton Avenue................	38	45
Fairmount Bridge	44	51
Mantua..........................	94	101
Belmont Avenue................	103	110
Hestonville	136	143
City Avenue.....................	214	221
Merion	240	247
Elm	278	285
Wynnewood	308	315
Ardmore.........................	352	359
Bryn Mawr	409	416
Rosemont	388	395
Villa Nova.......................	423	430
Union	423	430
Radnor	402	409
Edgewood Avenue..............	394	401
Wayne	398	405
Reeseville	488	495
Paoli.............................	527	534
Green Tree......................	536	543
Malvern..........................	539	546
Fraser	483	490
Glenlock.........................	446	453
Ship Bridge *....................	404	411
Walkertown.....................	381	388
E. B. & W. R. R. See Tab. II....	248	255
Downingtown	259	266
Gallaghersville	291	298
Thorndale.......................	306	313
Cain..............................	352	359
Coatesville (W.&R.R.R.) Tab.LVI.	373	380
Midway..........................	387	394
Pomeroy. P. & D. R. R. Tab. III.	476	483
Chandlers	482	489
Parkesburg	530	537
Summit †........................	551	558
Penningtonville.................	493	500
Christiana.......................	484	491
Summit ‡........................	566	573
Gap	552	559
Kinzers	461	468
Spindlers	397	404
Leamen Place	375	382
Gordonville	378	385
Fairview	378	385
Bird in Hand....................	352	359

* Intersection of Waynesburg Branch.
† West of Parkesburg.
‡ East of Gap Station.

STATIONS.		High Tide, Philad'a.	Mean Tide Atlantic Ocean.
Lancaster ‡		352	359
Dillerville Junction ‖	Columbia Line.	352	359
Rohrerstown §	Columbia Line.	345	352
Mountville	Columbia Line.	397	404
Columbia	Columbia Line.	244	251
Chiquies	Columbia Line.	248	255
Marietta	Columbia Line.	253	260
Shocks Mill	Columbia Line.	262	269
Bainbridge	Columbia Line.	264	271
Collins	Columbia Line.	278	285
Middletown Junction (*a*)	Columbia Line.	307	314
Landisv'e R. & C. R. R. (*b*). Tab. LVII		398	405
Salunga		396	403
Chiquies Bridge		344	351
Mount Joy (*c*)		359	366
Springville		383	390
Reams		432	439
Tunnel		472	479
Elizabethtown		450	457
Conewago		422	429
Middletown		307	314
Highspire		293	300
Harrisburg *		313	320
Susquehanna		335	342
Susquehanna Bridge		343	350
Marysville		343	350
N. C. R. R. Crossing † Tab.		342	349
Duncannon		349	356
Aqueduct		370	377
Bailys		380	387
Newport		388	395
Millerstown		401	408
Thompsontown		412	419
Tuscarora ¶		422	429
Mexico		426	433
Perryville		434	441
Mifflin		434	441
Black Log		455	462
Bixlers		475	482
Lewistown		491	498
M. & C. C. R. R. Crossing ‖‖ Tab. V.		492	499
Granville		491	498

‡ Bench Mark on Stone Wall, Lancaster Locomotive Works, 339.
‖ Junction of Columbia Branch, at Dillerville.
§ On Columbia Branch.
(*a*) Junction of Columbia Branch, at Middletown.
(*b*) Reading and Columbia R. R. Crossing, at Landisville.
(*c*) East side of R. R. Hotel.
* West line of depot 313.91. Curb stone at lamp post U. S. Hotel 313.54. West line of Lebanon Valley Depot 315.5. West line of State street 310.2.
† Northern Central R. R. Crossing.
¶ Bench Mark on top of Stone foundation west corner of Water Station 424.44.
‖‖ Junction at Mifflin and Centre County R. R.

STATIONS.	High Tide, Philad'a.	Mean Tide Atlantic Ocean.	
Anderson's	493	500	
Anderson's. Water Station	492	499	
McVeytown	515	522	
Manayunk	512	519	
Vineyard	541	548	
Newton Hamilton	592	599	
Mount Union. § E. B. T. Tab. VII.	590	597	
Jackstown	588	595	
Mapleton	586	593	
Mill Creek	597	604	
Huntingdon.* H.& B.T.Tab.VIII.	615	622	
Warrior Ridge	670	677	
Petersburg	671	678	
Sherman's Bridge †	692	699	
Barre Forge	717	724	
Tunnel ‡	754	761	
Spruce Creek	770	777	
Union Furnace	792	799	
Birmingham	859	866	
Tyrone Water Station	889	896	
Tyrone R.R. Tables XIII.XIV.XV.	900	907	
Tipton	983	990	
Fostoria	1022	1029	
Bells Mills R. R. Table XVIII	1053	1060	
Elizabeth Furnace	1072	1079	
Blair Furnace	1107	1114	
Altoona ‖ R.R. Tables XIX.-XXIII	1171	1178	
Kittanning	1587	1594	
Murdocks	1619	1626	
Alligrippus	1913	1920	
Bennington Furnace	2031	2038	
Tunnel ¶	2119	2126	
Gallitzin	2154	2161	
Cresson (*a*) E.&C.R.R.Tab.XXIV.	2010	2017	
Lillys	1880	1887	
Portage	1668	1675	
Wilmore	1550	1557	
Summit (*b*)	1562	1569	
Summerhill	1550	1557	
South Fork	1477	1485	
Viaduct (*c*)	1449	1456	

§ Junction of East Broad Top R. R. (narrow guage).

* West line of ticket office, crossing south track west to Huntingdon & Broad Top R. 613.0.

† Bench Mark on west end of bridge.

‡ West end of Spruce Creek Tunnel.

‖ West line of ticket office 1171. B. M. (Bench Mark) south-west corner, top step front door of ticket office 1174.

¶ B. M. at east end of Tunnel, on rough part of first course of stone above foundation.

(*a*) Switch to Ebensburgh and Cresson R. R. 2021.

(*b*) Pringles point.

(*c*) Bench Mark on N. W. corner west end of coping.

STATIONS.	High Tide, Philad'a.	Mean Tide Atlantic Ocean.	
Mineral Point	1407	1414	
Conemaugh	1218	1225	
Johnstown	1177	1184	
Sandy Hollow	1136	1143	
Conemaugh Furnace	1128	1135	
Nineveh	1134	1141	
New Florence	1069	1076	
Houstons	1049	1056	
Lockport	1047	1054	
Bolivar	1026	1033	
Blairsville Junction * Tab. XXV.	1106	1113	
Hillside	1122	1129	
Millwood	1148	1155	
Derry	1165	1172	
Lindorff's Summit	1178	1185	
St. Clair } Lig. R.R. Tab. XXIX.	1085	1092	
Latrobe } Lig. R.R. Tab. XXIX.	999	1006	
Beatty's	1066	1073	
Kearney's †	1041	1048	
Shanghai	1166	1173	
Carr's Tunnel ‡	1201	1208	
George's	1199	1206	
Greensburg‖S. W. P. RR. Tab. XXX.	1084	1091	
McGrau's Tunnel §	1156	1163	
Radebaughs	1143	1150	
Grapeville	1052	1059	
Penn	967	974	
Manor	935	942	
Shafton	893	900	
Irwin's. Y. R. R. Table XXXI.	877	884	
Larimer's	859	866	
Carpenter's	847	854	
Stewart's	784	791	
Wall's	744	751	
Springhill	742	749	
Turtle Creek	743	750	
Oak Hill	743	750	
Brinton's	750	757	
Braddock's	821	828	
Copeland	846	853	
Hawkins'	876	883	
Swiss Vale	915	922	
Edgewood	916	923	
Wilkinsburg	916	923	
Brushton	915	922	

* Intersection of Blairsville and Indiana Branch of Pa. R. R. with main line.

† Rogers' Summit 1201.8.

‡ East face of Tunnel.

‖ B. M. east face of Greensburg Tunnel on top of rough part of second course from bottom 'R' 1079.52.

§ West face of tunnel.

STATIONS.	High Tide, Philad'a.	Mean Tide Atlantic Ocean.	
Homewood	916	923	
Torrens	913	920	
East Liberty	911	918	
Roups'	875	882	
Shadyside	859	866	
Millvale	826	833	
Lawrenceville	773	780	
Pittsburgh *	738	745	

II. East Brandywine Railroad.

NOTE.—The levels on the East Brandywine and Waynesburg R. R. were furnished by Mr. W. H. Wilson, Consulting Engineer of the Pennsylvania R.R. The datum, or base of levels is ordinary high water in Schuylkill River, Philadelphia. Therefore 7 *feet are added in the second column to reduce to mean tide in the Atlantic Ocean.*

STATIONS.	High Tide, Philad'a.	Ocean Level.	
Downingtown Terminus. † Table I.	249	256	
Shelmeirs	239	246	
Dowlin's Forge	271	278	
Dorlan's	273	280	
Reed's Road	302	309	
Brooklyn	329	336	
Cornog's	354	361	
Springton	398	405	
Moorestown	436	443	
Barnestown	479	486	
Lewis Mills	535	542	
Cupola	556	563	
Forrest	564	571	
Dampman's	624	631	
W. & R. R. R. ‡ Table LVI.	666 ?	673 ?	
Buchanan's	665	672	
Lancaster Pike	689	696	
Waynesburg	721 ?	728 ?	
End of Track	734	741	

* West face of Union Passenger Depot, east side of Wayne Station 734.5. East side of Irwin street 729.7. East side of Duquesne street depot 725.4. Bench Mark at foot of lamp post south side of Liberty street, intersection with Water street 721.27.

Bench Mark on south side of base ring, of fire plug, north side of Penn street, intersection with Water street, 719.

† Junction with north track of the Pa. R. R. near Downingtown.

‡ Crossing Wilmington and Reading R. R.

III. Pennsylvania and Delaware R. R.

NOTE.—The elevations on the Pennsylvania and Delaware Railroad were obtained in the office of Mr. George W. Leuffer, C. E., of Philadelphia.

At Pomeroy Station, 43 miles of Philadelphia, this road joins the Pennsylvania R. R. Mr. Leuffer makes this point 472.9; Mr. Wilson 476.039. To Mr. Leuffer's levels in the first column are therefore added 3 feet to accord with the P. R. R. list, and an additional 7 feet to reduce to mean Atlantic tide level.

STATIONS.	High Tide, Philad'a.	Ocean Level.	
Pomorey Junction * Table I.	472.9	483	
Doe Run	364	374	
Pusey's Summit	460.	470	
Pennock's Summit	453	463	
Avondale ** Table	271.6	281.6	
Newark †	108	118	
Delaware R. R. Crossing ‡	76.2	86.2	
Delaware City	6.	16	

IV. York Branch P. R. R.

The levels on the York Branch of the Pennsylvania R. R. were copied from the profile in the office of the P. R. R. at Philadelphia.

In accordance with instructions of Mr. W. H. Wilson, 3′ was added to each elevation, as shown on the profile, in order to agree with the level of Columbia according to Pa. R. R.; and also 7 feet to reduce to mean Ocean level.

STATIONS.	High Tide, Philad'a.	Ocean Level.	
Columbia § Table I.	241.3	251.3	
Wrightsville	247.5	257.5	
Creitz Creek ‖	263.	273.	
Hellam	336	346	
Heistand's	327.2	337.2	
York (N. Central R. R.) Tab.	371.7	381.7	

* Junction with Pennsylvania R. R. at Pomeroy Station, 43 (42.2?) miles west of Philadelphia.

** Crossing the Philadelphia and Baltimore Central R. R.

† Crossing of the Delaware Railway Line.

‡ Crossing of the Philadelphia, Wilmington and Baltimore R. R.

§ Junction with the Columbia Branch of the Pa. R. R.

‖ Bench mark on east end of coping girder of bridge No. 3, over road and Creitz Creek.

V. *Mifflin and Centre Co. R. R.*

The levels of the Mifflin and Centre Co. Railroad were copied from a profile in the office of the Pennsylvania R. R. Co., at Philadelphia, furnished by Mr. W. H. Wilson, Consulting Engineer, Pennsylvania R. R.

The datum is that of the Pennsylvania R. R., 7 *feet added,* to reduce to mean Atlantic level, in the second column.

STATIONS.	Above Tide.	Ocean Level.	
Lewistown Junction*	492	499	
Logan	527	534	
Yeagertown	561	568	
Mann's	673	680	
Reedsville	695	702	
Honey Creek	807	814	
Nagney	849	856	
Milroy†	987	994	

VI. *Sunbury and Lewistown R. R.*

NOTE.—No records of this road could be obtained.

VII. *East Broad Top Narrow Gauge R. R.*

The levels on the East Broad Top R. R. (3 foot gauge), were copied from a profile in the office of the Company, at Orbisonia, by permission of Mr. A. W. Sims, Superintendent.

The datum of the profile is an assumed elevation, and has been reduced to tide level by reference to the Pennsylvania R. R. grade at Mount Union, 590′, with 7′ added to reduce to mean Atlantic Ocean level.

STATIONS.	Assumed Datum.	Ocean Level.	
Mount Union Junction ‡	810.65	597	
Morrison's Summit	828	615	
Aughwick Creek	773.60	560	
Shirleysburg	784.94	572	
Douglas Summit	811.24	598	
McMullen's Summit	882.74	669	
Orbisonia	837 62	624	
Jordan's Summit	922.22	709	
Scottsville	929.85	717	
Saltillo	994.70	781	
Moreland's Summit	1326.90	1114	
Sidling Hill	1445.47	1232	
Cole's Station	1572.06	1359	
Cook's Mill	1741.28	1528	
Cook's Station	1754.24	1541	
Coal Openings	1978.10	1765	
Robertsdale	1998.70	1785	
End of Road §	2030.02	1817	

* With the Pennsylvania R. R. near the Lewistown Station. Table I.

† Terminus in the Kishicoquillis Valley. This survey has been extended through the Seven Mountains to Bellefonte.

‡ East Broad Top R. R. connects with Pennsylvania R. R. at Mount Union.

§ On the plateau of the Broad Top Mountain in Huntingdon County.

VIII. Huntingdon and Broad Top R. R.

The levels on the Huntingdon and Broad Top R. R. and its Branches, were furnished by Mr. John Fulton, General Mining Engineer of the Cambria Iron Works at Johnstown, Pa.

The datum is 0 at grade on the Pennsylvania R. R. at Huntingdon. To this 614' are added, +7', to reduce all to mean Atlantic Ocean level.

This road has three coal branches up the three streams which drain the Broad Top Coal Region. It originally stopped at Everett; but has been continued to Bedford and Bridgeport under the name of the Bedford and Bridgeport Railroad. Table IX.

The elevations on the Bedford and Bridgeport R. R. were furnished by Mr. S. M. Prevost, Superintendent of the Bedford Division of the Pennsylvania R. R.

The datum 0 of this road was at grade of the Pennsylvania R. R at Huntingdon; which Mr Prevost called 610; while Mr. Wilson calls it 614. The difference of 4 feet has therefore, in the 2d column, been added to Mr. Prevost's figures, to make them agree with Mr. Wilson's figures, along the main line. The regular 7 feet addition has also been made in the second column to reduce to mean Atlantic Ocean level.

STATIONS.	Above Hunting-don.	Ocean Level.	
Huntingdon	000	621	
McConnellstown	56.2	677	
Pleasant Grove	127.2	748	
Marklesburg	167.6	789	
Coffee Run	250.6	872	
Rough and Ready	267.6	889	
Cove	300	921	
Fisher's Summit	253	874	
New Bridge	210.3	831	
Saxton (new depot)	228	849	
Riddlesburg	243.6	865	
Hopewell	277.3	898	
Piper's Run	326.3	947	
Brallier's Summit	487.3	1108	
Tatesville	475.3	1096	
Bloody Run Summit	613.3	1234	
Everett	497 3	1118	

IX. Continued as the Bedford and Bridgeport R. R.

Mount Dallas........(above tide)	1046	1053	
Cove Creek	1026	1033	
Lutzville	1038	1045	
Bedford	1055	1062	
Wolfsburg Summit	1111	1118	
Napier	1101	1108	
Mann's Choice	1129	1136	
Buffalo Summit	1349	1356	
Fossilville	1084	1091	
Bridgeport (*a*)	923	930	
Maryland State Line (*b*)	837	840	

(*a*) Not the Bridgeport of Clearfield County in Table XIV.

(*b*) Continued as Baltimore, Connellsville & Pittsburgh R. R. Branch of the Baltimore and Ohio R. R.

X. *Shoup's Run Branch of H. & B. T. R. R.*

Saxton (as above)	228	849	
Coalmont	488.8	1110	
Crawford	620.9	1242	
Old M. P	662 7	1284	
No. 3. Mine	784.5	1405	
Barnet Mine	767	1388	
Dudley Station	803.6	1425	
Blair's Mine	815.2	1436	
Moredale	1058.7	1680	
Water Station	1088	1709	
End of Track	1240.2	1861	

XI. *Six Mile Run Branch of H. & B. T. R. R.*

Riddlesburg (as above)	243.6	865	
" Coal Mine	340.9	962	
Coaldale	505.2	1126	
End of 3d Mile	573	1194	
End of 4th Mile	753	1374	
End of Track	795	1416	

XII. *Sandy Run Branch of H. & B. T. R. R.*

Hopewell (as above)	277.3	898	
End of Track	404	1025	

XIII. *Lewisburg, Centre and Spruce Creek R. R.*

NOTE.—The levels on the Lewisburg Centre and Spruce Creek R. R. were furnished by Mr. George W. Leuffer, Chief Engineer. Mr. Leuffer says, "I will remark that many of the Stations have, as yet, not been located. The tide levels are based upon a level furnished by A. B. Starr, Esq., Engineer of P. & E. R. R., of a point in abutment of Chilesquaque Bridge (of P. & E. R. R.), and this agrees so closely with the level of tide, as stated in printed table of Pennsylvania R. R. Co, of Tyrone City, that I am inclined to rely upon the levels I now enclose."

The first column, then, gives the figures of Mr. Leuffer.

The second column has 7 feet added to Mr. Leuffer's figures, on the supposition that his datum is Pennsylvania R. R. datum of high water at the Schuylkill Bridge.

The third column has 8 feet added (in addition, = 15 feet in all) to agree with the final mean Atlantic Ocean level assigned to Tyrone, in the Pennsylvania R. R. list, No. I.

STATIONS.	Above Tide.*	Ocean Level.†	Ocean Level.§	
P. & E. R.R. Junction (*a*)	447	454	462	
Lewisburg	451	458	466	
Biehl	503	510	518	
Vicksburg	514	521	529	
Mifflinburg	550	557	565	
Millmont	570	577	585	
Laurelton	592	599	607	
Tunnel (*b*)	944	951	959	
Fowler's	976	983	991	
Beaver Dam Tunnel	999	1006	1014	
Caburn (*c*)	1011	1018	1026	
Buchannon (*d*)	1044	1051	1059	
Duncan	1063	1070	1078	
Centre Hall	1257	1264	1272	
Summit (*e*)	1275	1282	1290	
Lemont (*f*)	987	994	1002	
Kelly (*g*)	1096	1103	1111	
Pinegrove	1221	1228	1236	
Shugarts	1116	1123	1131	
Lyon (Penna. Furnace)	1059	1066	1074	
Guyer (*h*)	1129	1136	1144	
Lowrie (*i*)	1094	1101	1109	
Miller (*j*)	1055	1062	1070	
Tyrone (*k*) (I)	892	899	907	

XIV. Tyrone and Clearfield R. R.

The elevations on the Tyrone and Clearfield R. R. were copied from a profile in the office of the Pennsylvania R. R. Co. in Philadelphia. The datum is a point 60′ below Tyrone, or as it appears on the profile elevation at Tyrone + 840′. Mr. W. H. Wilson is authority for adding 60′ to each elevation as shown on the profile.

In the second column seven feet are added to reduce to mean Atlantic Ocean Level.

---

* High tide, Schuylkill River, at Philadelphia?

† Calculated from the Lewisburg end.

§ Adjusted to the Pennsylvania R. R. record at the Tyrone end.

(*a*) Junction with Philadelphia and Erie R. R

(*b*) Through Paddy's Mountain.

(*c*) Forks of Penn's Creek.

(*d*) Mouth of Muddy Run.

(*e*) Summit of Penn's Valley, Head of Penn's Creek, and Head of Spring Creek, which enters Bald Eagle Creek after passing Bellefonte.

(*f*) End of Nittany Mountain.

(*g*) State Agricultural College.

(*h*) Half Moon Gap.

(*i*) At Warrior's Mark.

(*j*) Logan's Run.

(*k*) L. C. & Sp. Cr. R. R. here connects with the Pennsylvania R. R.

STATIONS.	Above Tide.	Ocean Level.	
Tyrone (Pennsylvania R. R.)..(I)	900	907	
Bald Eagle R. R. Junction.......	977	984	
Vanscoyoc....................	1410	1417	
Gardners	1561	1568	
Mt. Pleasant..................	1767	1774	
Emigh's Summit (*a*)...........	2033	2040	
Sandy Ridge..................	1915	1922	
Powelton	1791	1798	
Osceola Branch R. R...........	1481	1488	
Dunbar.......................	1446	1453	
Moshannon Creek..............	1443	1450	
Steiner's Mill.................	1421	1428	
Philipsburg	1415	1422	
Blue Ball.....................	1513	1520	
Shimmels.....................	1634	1641	
Wallacetown..................	1675	1682	
Turner's Summit...............	1735	1742	
Moravian Run.................	1731	1738	
Ross' Summit..................	1744	1751	
Smael's Summit................	1709	1716	
Camp Hummel..................	1743	1750	
Bigler........................	1655	1662	
Woodland.....................	1465	1472	
Roaring Run..................	1420	1427	
Leonard's Point...............	1299	1306	
Clearfield Creek...............	1133	1140	
Sharon's Run..................	1105	1112	
Liberty Spring................	1096	1103	
Clearfield.....................	1096	1103	
Goodfellow's Bridge............	1103	1110	
Spackman's Bluff...............	1110	1117	
Susquehanna River.............	1117	1124	
Hog Back.....................	1119	1126	
Hartshorn's Run...............	1125	1132	
Curwensville	1134	1141	
Anderson's Creek (*b*)...........	1144	1151	
Anderson's Creek (*c*)...........	1159	1166	
Bridgeport (*d*).................	1183	1190	

XV. Bald Eagle Valley R. R.

The elevations on the Bald Eagle Valley R. R. were copied from a profile in the office of the Pennsylvania R R. Company, at Philadelphia. The datum is the same as that of the P. R. R.

In the second column seven feet are added to reduce to mean Atlantic Ocean Level.

(*a*) Allegheny Mountain Summit.
(*b*) First Crossing.
(*c*) Second Crossing.
(*d*) Not the Bridgeport of Bedford County in Table IX.

STATIONS.	Above Tide.	Ocean Level.	
Tyrone (as above)	900	907	
Spring Run	888	895	
Dallas Street	921	928	
Sinking Run	923	930	
Little B. E. Creek	940	947	
Bald Eagle	1051	1058	
L. B. E. Bridge	1065	1072	
Summit	1103	1110	
Hannah	1050	1057	
Port Matilda (*a*)	1000	1007	
B. E. Creek Bridge	917	924	
Martha	905	912	
Julian	844	851	
Dick's Run	794	801	
Unionville	775	782	
Snow Shoe R. R. (XVI)	715	722	
Milesburg (XVII)	693	700	
Bald Eagle Canal	664	671	
Holters'	644	651	
Mount Eagle	655	662	
Bald Eagle Plank Road	658	665	
Howard	672	679	
Eagleville	628	635	
Beach Creek	607	614	
Mill Hall	566	573	
Lock Haven Junction (*b*)	548	555	

(*a*) Main Street.
(*b*) Junction with the Philadelphia and Erie R. R.

XVI. Bellefonte and Snow Shoe R. R.

The levels on the Bellefonte and Snow Shoe R. R. were furnished by Mr. I. L. Sommerville, Resident Engineer. The datum is that of the Pennsylvania R. R.

In the second column seven feet are added to reduce to mean Atlantic Ocean Level.

STATIONS.	Above Tide.	Ocean Level.	
Bellefonte (XVII)	737	744	
Bald Eagle R. R. Junction (XV)	715	722	
Gum Stump	1013	1020	
Summit (*a*)	1728	1735	
Beach Creek (*b*)	1542	1549	
Beach Creek (*c*)	1592	1599	
Snow Shoe	1565	1572	
Middle Coal bed (*d*)	1599	1606	

(*a*) Allegheny Mountain summit.
(*b*) *Level of water* in Beach Creek.
(*c*) Level of rail over the water.
(*d*) Middle coal bed at the Company's mines at Coal Hill.

XVII. *Bellefonte Branch.*

The levels on the Bellefonte Branch were copied from a profile in the office of the Pennsylvania R. R. Company, at Philadelphia, and have the datum of the P. R. R. to which are added seven feet to reduce to mean Atlantic Ocean Level, in the second column.

STATIONS.	Above Tide.	Ocean Level.	
Milesburg (*a*)..............(XV)	693	700	
B. E. V. Plank Road............	692	699	
Bellefonte................(XVI)	737	744	

XVIII. *Bell's Gap (N. G.) R. R.*

The elevations on the Bell's Gap Narrow Gauge R. R. (3 feet) were furnished by Mr. Jos. Ramsey, Jr., Superintendent.

The datum for the first column is 0 at Pennsylvania R. R. grade at Bell's Mills Station. To which are added 1053′ from Table I for the second column, and 7′ for the third column, to reduce to mean Atlantic Ocean Level.

STATIONS.	Bell's Mills.†	Corrected Tide.	Ocean Level.	
Bell's Mills Junction (I).	0	1053	1060	
Roots'.................	162	1215	1222	
Collier	581.6	1635	1642	
Point Lookout..........	854.6	1908	1915	
Lloyd's Junction (*a*) ...	1107.4	2160	2167	
Lloyd's Station	1119.7	2173	2180	
Summit (*b*)............	1240.5	2294	2301	
Five Foot Coal (*c*)......	——	2116	2123	
Figart's	1048	2101	2108	
Vanscoyoc.............	935	1988	1995	
Crees Summit..........	797	1850	1857	
Hollen's (*d*)	582	1635	1642	
Three Foot Coal........	——	1667	1674	
Five Foot Coal	——	1727	1734	
Van Ormer's (*e*)........	352.3	1405	1412	
Three Foot Coal........	——	1475	1482	
Fallen Timber	362.	1415	1422	

(*a*) Junction with the Bald Eagle Valley R. R.

(*a*) Elevation of 5 foot coal bed at the mouth of gangway.

(*b*) Allegheny Mountain. Bench Mark, Summit of Mountain.

(*c*) Level of the 5 foot coal bed under the Bench Mark.

(*d*) Elevation at this point of the 3′ vein, 1667′; of the 5′ vein, 1727′.

(*e*) Elevation of *Water in Clearfield Creek.* The elevation of the 3′ vein here is 1475.

XIX. Hollidaysburg Branch P. R. R.

The levels on the Hollidaysburg Branch of the Pennsylvania R.R. were copied from a profile in the office of the P. R. R. Company, at Philadelphia.

The datum being mean high tide at the Schuylkill Bridge, seven feet are added in the second column to reduce the mean Atlantic Ocean Level.

STATIONS.	Above Tide.	Ocean Level.	
Altoona (Pennsylvania R. R.)..(I)	1172	1179	
Allegheny......................	1145	1152	
Eldorado	1086	1093	
Canon's	1059	1066	
Duncansville	983	990	
Hollidaysburg ....(XX)	946	953	
End of Line (*a*)	937	944	

(*a*) 3400′ beyond the station marked Hollidaysburg.

XX. Williamsburg Branch P. R. R.

The levels on the Williamsburg Branch, the Morrison's Cove Branch, the Bloomfield Branch, and the Springfield Branch of the Pennsylvania R. R., were copied from profiles in the office of the Pennsylvania R. R. Company, at Philadelphia.

The datum being mean high tide at the Schuylkill Bridge, seven feet are added to reduce to mean Atlantic Ocean Level.

The Williamsburg Branch R. R. has been substituted for the old State Canal, long since vacated, from Frankstown to Williamsburg, and shows the fall of the Juniata River.

STATIONS.	Above Tide.	Ocean Level.	
Graysport (*a*)....................	947	954	
Hollidaysburg ....(XIX)	935	942	
Brush Run......................	1026	1033	
Juniata River (*b*)	911	918	
Reese Station	896	903	
Clapper's Run	894	901	
Koofer's Run	886	893	
Juniata River (*c*)	886	893	
Pike Ponds	878	885	
Flowing Spring	874	881	
Springfield R.R. Junc. (*d*) (XXIII)	874	881	
Williamsburg	840	847	

(*a*) Bench Mark on step of ladies' waiting room, Graysport passenger station, 946.60′

(*b*) Frankstown or Main Branch of the Juniata River.

(*c*) Frankstown or Main Branch of the Juniata River.

(*d*) Springfield Branch.

XXI. Morrison's Cove Branch P. R. R.

STATIONS.	Above Tide.	Ocean Level.	
Hollidaysburg .... (XIX)	936	943	
Draw Bridge	935	942	
Juniata River (*e*)	935	942	
Reservoir	960	967	
Catfish	961	968	
Riddle's Lane	966	973	
Brooks Mill	999	1006	
McKee's Gap (*f*)	1029	1036	
Martha Furnace	1047	1054	
Hammond's	1126	1133	
Roaring Spring Junction.. (XXII)	1199	1206	
Erb's Summit	1347	1354	
Martinsburg Junction	1337	1344	
Martinsburg..................	1359	1366	
Henrietta Junction..............	1384	1391	
Mathew's Summit	1465	1472	
Nicodemus' Summit	1425	1432	
Clover Creek	1385	1392	
Henrietta Ore Bank	1402	1409	
End of Road (*g*)...............	1415	1422	

XXII. Bloomfield Branch P. R. R.

STATIONS.	Above Tide.	Ocean Level.	
Roaring Spring (*h*)........(XXI)	1196	1203	
Trestle, No. 1	1214	1221	
Trestle, No. 2..................	1351	1358	
Bloomfield (*i*)	1453	1460	

XXIII. Springfield Branch P. R. R.

STATIONS.	Above Tide.	Ocean Level.	
Williamsburg R. R. Junc....(XX)	874	881	
Trestle, No. 1..................	961	968	
Goods..........................	999	1006	
Davis Summit	1372	1379	
8th Mile Post (*j*)...............	1367	1374	

(*e*) Frankstown Branch of the Juniata River.

(*f*) Through Dunning's Mountain.

(*g*) In Leather Cracker Cove, the southern end of Morrison's Cove.

(*h*) Junction of this branch with Morrison's Cove Branch R. R. XXI.

(*i*) Iron Mines and Furnaces.

(*j*) This R. R. ascends from the Juniata River to the Springfield Ore Mines in Canoe Valley, the northeast prolongation of Morrison's Cove.

XXIV. *Ebensburg and Cresson R. R.*

The elevations on the Ebensburg and Cresson Railroad were copied from a profile in the office of the Pennsylvania R. R. Company, in Philadelphia.

The datum is mean high water at the Schuylkill Bridge, to which are added seven feet to reduce to mean Atlantic Ocean Level.

STATIONS.	Above Tide.	Ocean Level.	
Cresson R. R. Junction (*a*)....(I)	2021	2028	
Plank Road Crossing............	2032	2039	
Lilly..........................	2023	2030	
O'Harra........................	2008	2015	
Durbin.........................	1920	1927	
Sander's.......................	2012	2019	
Bradley's......................	2111	2118	
Dam (*b*)......................	1953	1960	

(*a*) The Junction with Pa. R. R. is not *at* Cresson 2010′ (2017′) but *near* Cresson 2021′ (2028).

(*b*) This is the last point on the profile where the elevation is given.

XXV. *Blairsville and Indiana Branch P. R. R.*

The elevations on the Blairsville and Indiana Branch of the Pennsylvania R. R. were taken from a profile in the office of the P. R. R. Company, at Philadelphia.

The datum is high tide Schuylkill River, at the Philadelphia Market Street Bridge. To this seven feet are added in the second column to reduce to mean Atlantic Ocean Level.

STATIONS.	Above Tide.	Ocean Level.	
R. R. Junction (*a*)............(I)	1104	1111	
Pennsylvania Canal.............	958	965	
R. R. Junction (*b*)............	970	977	
Blairsville (*c*)...............	1004	1011	
Smith's Summit.................	1096	1103	
Wier's Run.....................	963	970	
Black Lick.....................	956	963	
Water Station..................	959	966	
Black Lick Bridge..............	1075	1082	
Doty's Bridge..................	1004	1011	
Rough's........................	1021	1028	
Saw Mill Run...................	1009	1016	
Bell's Mill's Run..............	1025	1032	
Phillips' Summit...............	1037	1044	
Kissinger's Summit.............	1048	1055	
Two Lick Creek.................	1037	1044	
Reed's.........................	1138	1145	
Indiana Terminus...............	1304	1311	

(*a*) With the Main line Pennsylvania R. R. on the side of Chestnut Ridge, high above the bed of the river.

(*b*) With the Indiana and Blairsville Branch

(*c*) Market Street Station, in Blairsville.

XXVI. *West Penn R. R.*

The levels of the West Penn R. R. were copied from a profile in the office of the Pennsylvania R. R. Company, at Philadelphia.

The datum is mean high tide in the Schuylkill River, at Philadelphia. In the second column seven feet are added to reduce to mean Atlantic Ocean Level.

This Railroad follows down the valley of the Kishkiminitas from Blairsville to Freeport, sometimes using the bed of the old State Canal.

STATIONS.	Above Tide.	Ocean Level.	
Blairsville (*a*)..............XXV	1004	1011	
Livermore......................	938	945	
Saltzburg (*b*)	884	891	
Fairbank's (*c*)............XXVII	926	933	
Helma	1010	1017	
Salina..........................	948	955	
North West....................	887	894	
Roaring Run	823	830	
Apollo	816	823	
Townsend's Summit	880	887	
Grinder's	820	827	
Hill's Mill......................	773	780	
A. V. R. R. Crossing (*d*)........	778	785	
Freeport (*e*)............XXVIII	763	770	
Sligo	768	775	
Karn's	761	768	
Natrona........................	761	768	
Tarentum	750	757	
Bailey's Run	746	753	
Springdale	742	749	
Harmersville	736	743	
Fairview	734	741	
Ross	738	745	
Sharpsburg (*f*)	732	739	
Bennett's......................	734	741	
Duquesne Borough..............	734	741	
Allegheny City (*g*)............	736	743	
Allegheny City (*h*)	738	745	
Allegheny City (*i*)............	736	743	
Terminus (*j*)	734	741	

(*a*) Market Street Station, Blairsville.

(*b*) Market Street, Saltzburg.

(*c*) Coal R. R. here connects, see next table XXVII.

(*d*) Crossing Allegheny Valley R. R.

(*e*) Second Street, Freeport.

(*f*) Main Street, Sharpsburg.

(*g*) Sycamore Street, Allegheny City.

(*h*) Chestnut Street, Allegheny City.

(*i*) East Lane, Allegheny City.

(*j*) Opposite Pittsburgh and connecting with the Pittsburgh, Fort Wayne and Chicago R. R. lines.

XXVII. Branch of W. P. R. R.

The levels on the Branch of the West Penn Railroad from Fairbank's Station to the Coal Mines were furnished by Mr. George W. Leuffer, C. E. The datum 0 is at grade of W. P. R. R., Fairbank's Station.

STATIONS.	Above Tide.	Ocean Level.	
Fairbank's Junction.......XXVI	926	933	
Grade near Mines...............	1111	1118	
Bottom of Coal Bed.............	1133	1140	

XXVIII. Butler Branch W. P. R. R.

The levels on the Butler Branch Extension of the West Penn R. R. were furnished by Mr. Antes Snyder, Engineer, Springdale, Allegheny County, Pa.

There is an unexplained difference of 29.5 feet between the Butler Branch R. R. grade and the West Penn R. R. grade at Freeport, where they ought to be the same.

Another list was obtained from Mr. J. M. C. Creighton, differing very slightly from Mr. Snyder's; but still leaving *an unexplained difference of 27 feet at Freeport.*

The second column in the first table gives Mr. Snyder's levels *let down 29½ feet*, and in the second table Mr. Creighton's levels let down 27 feet.

The third column has seven feet added to reduce to mean Atlantic Ocean Level.

The datum of both tables is called "Mid Tide" at Philadelphia, which would require an addition of only 3.349 feet (instead of 7) to his original figures. See foot note on page 64. But this "Mid-Tide" may be a mistake for the "Mean High Tide" of the Pennsylvania R. R. Company's datum and is so taken.

STATIONS.	Mid Tide Philada.	2d Column.	Ocean Level.	
Freeport Junc....XXVI	792.5 †	763 ‡	770	
Buffalo	792.5	763	770	
Monroe................	865.5	836	843	
Sarver's................	1056	1026.5	1034.5	
Saxon..................	1254.5	1225	1232	
Delano	1255.5	1226	1233	
Dilke's................	1335	1305.5	1313.5	
Summit ‖	1344.5	1315	1322	
Great Belt City.........	1286.5	1257	1264	
Summit §..............	1328	1298.5	1306.5	
Herman................	1323.5	1394	1301	
Bunker's	1285.5	1256	1263	
Butler ....A	1031.5	1002	1009	

† Levels furnished by Mr. Antes Snyder.

‡ Elevation on profile of West Penn R. R. at Freeport.

‖ West of Dilke's.

§ East of Herman.

STATIONS.	Mid Tide Philada.	2d Column.	Ocean Level.	
Freeport Junc....XXVI	790 †	763 ‡	770	
Buffalo	788	761	768	
Harbison...............	824	797	804	
Monroe................	862	835	842	
Sarver's................	1052	1025	1032	
Saxonberg..............	1227	1200	1207	
Delano	1252	1225	1232	
Dilke's................	1337	1310	1317	
Great Belt..............	1285	1258	1265	
Herman...............	1318.50	1291	1298	
Bunker................	1288.38	1261	1268	
Butler. ....B	1030	1003	1010	

XXIX. Ligonier Valley R. R

The levels on the Ligonier Valley R. R. were copied from notes in possession of Mr. George L. Miller, C. E., Pittsburgh, Pa. The datum is Pennsylvania R. R. at Latrobe. To which add 1144 for high tide at Philadelphia.

STATIONS.	Above Tide.	Ocean Level.	
Ligonier........................	1144	1151	
Mill Creek.....(Surface of water)	1131	1138	
Coal Pit Run..................	1132	1139	
Schriner's Run.................	1127	1134	
Turnpike Crossing (*a*)...........	1123	1130	
Butler Milk Falls (*b*)............	1123	1130	
Baker's Saw Mills (*c*)...........	1117	1124	
Little Rock Hollow.............	1096	1103	
Big Rock Hollow...............	1080	1107	
Kellog's Hollow.................	1068	1075	
Iron Ore (*d*).....................	1040	1047	
Johnson's Forge................	1036	1043	
Derry Road Crossing............	1030	1037	
Mitchell's Run (*e*)....	1029	1036	

XXX. S. W. Pennsylvania R. R.

The levels of the South West Pennsylvania R. R. were furnished by Mr. G. W. Leuffer, Engineer.

The datum or base of levels is ordinary High Tide at Philadelphia.

† Elevations furnished by Mr. J. M. C. Creighton, Superintendent, West Penn. Division, Pennsylvania R. R.

‡ Elevation on profile of West Penn R. R. at Freeport.

(*a*) Greensburg and Stoystown.

(*b*) Loyalhanna Creek.

(*c*) At a point opposite Baker's Saw Mills.

(*d*) Out-crop of iron ore on line of R. R. 7 miles from Ligonier and 3 miles from Latrobe.

(*e*) Near Latrobe on the Pennsylvania R. R. Table I.

STATIONS.	Above Tide.	Ocean Level.	
Greensburg Junction (*a*)........I	1093	1100	
East Greensburg.................	1055	1062	
Huffs..........................	994	1001	
County Home...................	972	979	
Fosterville....................	960	967	
Youngwood.....................	950	957	
Jack's Run,....................	947	954	
Paintersville..................	945	952	
Sewickley Creek................	936	943	
Hunker's.	938	945	
Bethany........................	1044	1051	
Tarr's.........................	1092	1099	
Stoner's Summit................	1138	1145	
Hawk Eye.......................	1060	1067	
Scottdale......................	1035	1042	
Jacob's Creek..................	1027	1034	
Everson........................	1027	1034	
Valley Works...................	1068	1075	
Pennsville Summit..............	1086	1093	
Pennsville.....................	1047	1054	
Davidson.......................	891	898	
Connellsville..................	908	915	

(*a*) Junction with Pennsylvania R. R. near Greensburg.

XXXI. Yohiogheny R. R.

The elevations on the Yohiogheny R. R. were copied from notes in the possession of Mr. John F. Wolf, Engineer Pennsylvania Gas Coal Co., Irwin's Station, Westmoreland County, Pa.

The datum is Pennsylvania R. R. at:

STATIONS.	Above Tide.	Ocean Level.	
Irwin's Stat. P. R. R. (*a*).......1	877	884	
Shaft No. 2....................	986	993	
Tunnel.........................	1104	1111	
Chamber's......	1075	1082	
McGrew's.......................	974	981	
Millgrove..	926	933	
Little Sewickley (*b*)............	797	804	
Marchand's (*c*)..................	763	770	
Yohiogheny (*d*)..................	776	783	
Sewickley Station (*e*)...........	773	780	
R. R. Junction (*f*)..............	761	768	

(*a*) Junction with Pennsylvania R. R. at Irwin's Station.
(*b*) First Crossing Little Sewickley Creek.
(*c*) Yohiogheny Mine, No. 1, Shaft No. 3, elevation of Coal, 720′.4 above Tide.
(*d*) Yohiogheny Mine, No. 2, elevation of Coal 776′.4 above Tide.
(*e*) Mine No. 4, elevation of Coal opening at this point 800′.4 above Tide.
(*f*) Junction with Pittsburgh and Connellsville R. R.

II. READING SERIES.

L. *Philadelphia and Reading R. R.*

The elevations at the following points on the Philadelphia and Reading Railroad and Branches, were furnished by Mr. Wm. Lorenz, Chief Engineer.

The number of stations given in the tables, are few, but no others could be obtained.

The datum is *mid tide* at Philadelphia.

To this must be added 3.349 feet to reduce to Atlantic Ocean Level.

STATIONS.	Mean Tide.	Ocean Level.	
Philadelphia (*a*)			
Nicetown Summit (*b*)..,......LI	111	114	
Belmont			
West Falls......................			
Pencoyd			
West Manayunk..................			
Mill Creek......................			
West Spring Mill			
West Conshohocken...............			
Swede Furnace			
Bridgeport (*c*)...............LII			
Merion..........................			
Port Kennedy (*c*)............LII			
Valley Forge			
Perkiomen Junction (*d*)......LIV			
Phœnixville (*e*).............LIII	105	108	
Mingo			
Royer's Ford....................			
Limerick			
Pottstown (*f*)...............LV	146	149	
Douglassville			
Monocacy			
Birdsboro (*g*).................	170	173	
Exeter			
Neversink.......................			
Reading (*h*)...LVI, LVII, LVIII, LIX........................	264	267	
Tuckerton.......................			
Leesport........................	292	297	
Mohrsville			
Shoemakersville			
Hamburg.........................	361	364	
Port Clinton (*i*)...........LXII	397	400	
Auburn (*j*)..................LXIII	457	460	
Landingville....................			
Schuylkill Haven (*k*)......( )	520	523	
Mount Carbon....................	591	594	
Pottsville (*l*) LXVI	603	606	

a Richmond Street Bridge, near the Coal Depots on the Delaware River.

b In Philadelphia, near the Germantown Road. The Germantown R. R.

LI. Germantown and Norristown Branch P. & R. R. R.

STATIONS.	Mean Tide.	Ocean Level.	
Philadelphia (*a*)................I	39	42	
Nicetown (*b*)..................	132	135	
Columbia Avenue......See below			
New York Junction..			
Tioga..........................			
Wayne			
Fisher's.......................			
Duey's (or Wistar Street)........			
Shoemaker's....................			
Church Lane....................			
Germantown Depot (*m*)..........	212	215	
Chestnut Hill	404	407	
Philadelphia....................			
Columbia Avenue .....See above	39	42	
New York Junction.............			
East Falls.....................			
School Lane....................			
Wissahickon			
Schur's........................			
Manayunk			
Springfield.....................			
Shawmont......................			
Princeton			
Lafayette.......................			
Spring Mill			
Conshohocken			
Potts Landing..................			
Magee's........................			
Norristown (*n*)..............CIII	62	65	

crosses the P. & R. R. R. in Nicetown on a bridge at an elevation of 132 (135). feet; but not at this summit. Table LI.

c Norristown opposite Bridgeport is given in this list as 62 (65.) See Table LI. Bridgeport is at the Junction of the Chester Valley R. R. See Table LII. R. R. to King of Prussia; no levels furnished.

d Perkiomen R. R.

e Pickering Valley R. R.

f Colebrookdale R. R.

g Wilmington and Reading R. R.

h Lebanon Valley R. R. Reading and Columbia R. R. East Penn R. R.

i Little Schuylkill R. R.

j Schuylkill and Susquehanna R. R.

k West Branch R. R.

l Mill Creek R. R. Schuylkill Valley R. R.

---

a Depot at the corner of 9th and Green Streets.

b Crosses the P. & R. R. R. on a bridge, but not at the Nicetown Summit mentioned in Table L.

m Probably the old Depot.

n The N. Penn. R. R. level, Stony Creek branch, is 50 (62 Ocean level).

LII. Chester Valley Railroad

The levels on the Chester Valley Railroad, were furnished by Mr. W. H. Holstein, Secretary of the Chester Valley Railroad Company.

The road connects with the Philadelphia and Reading Railroad at Bridgeport, and with the Pennsylvania R. R. at Downingtown.

The base of the levels is *mid tide* at Philadelphia. Add 3.349 to reduce to Ocean level.

STATIONS.	Mean Tide.	Ocean Level.	
Bridgeport (*a*)................L	73	76	
Shainlines....................	133	136	
Henderson's....................	162	165	
King of Prussia................	187	190	
Centreville	199	202	
Gardens........................	222	225	
Howellville....................	218	221	
Paoli Road.....................	235	238	
Cedar Hollow..................	243	246	
Lee's..........................	276	279	
Valley Store...................	292	295	
Mill Lane	312	315	
White Horse...................	336	339	
Exton..........................	321	324	
Oakland........................	298	301	
Baldwin's......................	296	299	
Downingtown (*b*).............I	264	267	

LIII. Pickering Valley R. R.

Of this line only one level was furnished.

Datum (Reading R. R.) mean tide at Philadelphia. Add 3.349 for Ocean level.

STATIONS.	Mean Tide.	Ocean Level.	
Phœnixville L	(105)	(108)	
French Creek..................			
Kimberton			
Pikeland			
Chester Springs			
Cambria........................			
Byer's Eagle Summit............	450	453	

a Opposite Norristown, Table L.

b On the Pennsylvania R. R.

LIV. Perkiomen R. R.

STATIONS.	Mean Tide.		
Perkiomen Junction (*a*)........L			
Oaks...........................			
Doe Run			
Yerke's			
Collegeville...	151	154	
Rahn's			
Grater's Ford			
Skippack			
Schwenksville	149	152	
Green Land	245	248	
Emaus Junction (*b*)..........LXI			

a Reading R. R.
b East Penn R. R.

LV. Colebrookdale R. R.

STATIONS.	Mean Tide.	Ocean Level.	
Pottstown (*a*)...............L	(146)	(149)	
Glasgow			
Manatawny......................			
Iron Stone			
Colebrookdale			
Boyertown	388	391	
New Berlin			
Bechtelsville			
Mt. Pleasant...................	466	469	
Rittenhouse Gap................			
Alburtis (*b*)................LXI	(427)	(430)	

a Reading R. R.
b East Penn R. R.

LVI. Wilmington and Reading R. R.

STATIONS.	Mean Tide.	Ocean Level.	
Reading.......................L	(264)	(267)	
Birdsboro (*a*)................L	(170)	(173)	
Springfield....................			
Coatesville (*b*)...............I			
Chadd's Ford (*c*)...............			
Wilmington (*d*)................			

a Junction with Philadelphia and Reading R. R.
b Crosses Pennsylvania R. R.
c Crosses Philadelphia and Baltimore R. R.
d Connects with Philadelphia, Wilmington and Baltimore R. R.

LVI. Wilmington and Reading R. R.

These levels of the Wilmington and Reading R. R. were furnished by Mr. E. Collings, Superintendent.

The datum, or base of levels, is low tide at Wilmington, Del. Relation of Ocean Level to this datum is unknown.

STATIONS.	Low Tide.	Ocean Level.	
Birdsboro Junction (*a*).........L	173	(173)	
Hampton........................	223		
White Bear......................	349		
Geigertown......................	432		
Cold Run........................	525		
Joanna..........................	627		
Springfield.....................	645		
Conestoga.......................	647		
Isabella........................	639		
E. B. & W. R. R. Crossing (*b*)..II	647		
Beaver..........................	603		
Honeybrook......................	596		
Manor...........................	572		
Hibernia........................	530		
Brandywine......................	556		
Coatesville (*c*)...............I	315.		
Modena..........................	278		
Mortonville.....................	260		
Laurel..........................	241		
Embréiville.....................	231		
Glen Hall.......................	218		
Northbrook......................	209		
Seeds...........................	195		
Lenape..........................	183		
Pecopson........................	180		
Chadd's Ford....................	175		
Smith Bridge....................	209		
Centre..........................	263		
Dupont's........................	282		
Wilmington......................	12	(12)	

a Junction with Philadelphia and Reading R. R. at Birdsboro, Berks County, Pennsylvania.

b Junction with E. Brandywine and Waynesburg R. R., Chester County, Pa.

c The Pennsylvania R. R. track on bridge just west of Coatesville Station is 62′ higher than track on W. & R. R. R. The elevation on Pennsylvania R. R. at the point where it crosses the W. & R. R. R. is 374′ above tide. By deducting 62′ according to Pennsylvania R. R. datum the elevation would be 312′. The datum of the Pennsylvania R. R. is high tide in Schuylkill River. The datum of W. & R. R. R. is low tide at Wilmington.

LVII. Lebanon Valley R. R.

STATIONS.	Mean Tide.	Ocean Level.	
Reading (*a*)..................L	(264)	(267)	
Schuylkill Bridge..............	262	265	
Sinking Springs (*b*).......LVIII	(341)	(344)	
Wernersville....................	376	379	
Heidelburg......................	376	379	
Robesonia.......................	428	431	
Sand Holes Summit...............	450	453	
Womelsdorf......................	433	436	
Smiths'.........................	425	428	
Missimer's......................	425	428	
Richland........................	420	423	
Myerstown.......................	460	463	
Prescott........................	503	506	
Avon............................	467	470	
Lebanon.........................	456	459	
C. R. R. Junction (*c*)..........LX	444	447	
L. & T. R. R. Junction (*d*)...LIX	439	442	
Annville........................	436	439	
Palmyra.........................	443	446	
Spring Creek....................	384	387	
Hummelstown.....................	360	363	
Swatara Creek...................	355	358	
Swatara Hills Summit............	428	431	
Rutherford's....................	425	428	
Paxton..........................	363	366	
Harrisburg (*e*)..................I	308	311	

a Reading R. R.
b Reading and Columbia R. R.
c Cornwall R. R. Junction.
d Lebanon and Tremont R. R. Junction.
e West Line of Lebanon Valley Depot, Harrisburg, which, however, according to Pennsylvania R. R. Table I, is 315.5; probably more correct than 308.

LVIII. Reading and Columbia R. R.

STATIONS.	Above Tide.	Ocean Level.	
Reading........................L	(264)	(267)	
Sinking Springs (*a*)........LVII	341	344	
Deep Cut (*b*).....................	566	569	
Fitztown........................			
Reinhold's......................			
Union...........................			
Ephrata.........................	378	381	

a Junction with the Lebanon Valley Road.
b South Mountain Summit.

LVIII. *Reading and Columbia R. R.*—CONTINUED.

STATIONS.	Above Tide.	Ocean Level.	
Rothville Summit (*c*)............	401	404	
Litiz........................			
Manheim......................			
Sellers......................			
Lancaster Junction.............			
Landisville (*d*)................I	397	400	
Bruckhart's..................			
Ironville....................			
Kauffman's...................			
Chestnut Hill Summit...........	582	585	
Columbia (*e*).................I	257	260	

c This summit comes in *somewhere* between Ephrata and Landisville.

d Crosses Pennsylvania R. R. *on grade.* It is given as 398 (405) in Table I, = a difference in the *Ocean Level* column of (5) feet.

e The Pennsylvania *Ocean Level* grade here is (251) at the depot on the street, lower down on the hill slope.

LIX. *Lebanon and Tremont R. R.*

STATIONS.	Mean Tide.	Ocean Level.	
Lebanon Junction (*a*).......LVII	(439)	(442)	
Heilmansdale.................	505	508	
Bunker Hill..................			
Jonestown....................			
Union Forge..................			
Swatara Gap..................			
Murray.......................			
Mifflin......................			
Irving.......................			
S. & S. R. R. Junc. (*b*)....LXIII	491	494	
Pinegrove....................			
L. G. Ex. R. R. Junc. (*c*)....(..)			
Tremont (R. R. Junc.) (*d*)...(..)			
Donaldson....................	901	904	
Kalmia Colliery..............	1128	1131	

LX. *Cornwall R. R.*

NOTE.—The levels on the Cornwall Railroad were copied from a profile furnished by Mr. A. Wilhelm, President of the Company.

Reading R. R. datum, Mean Tide at Philadelphia. Add 3.319 feet for ocean level.

Lines have been surveyed south to Mount Hope, and to Manheim.

a Lebanon Valley R. R.

b Schuylkill and Susquehanna R. R.

c Lorberry Gap Extension R. R.

d Mine Hill R. R.; Lyken's Valley R. R.

STATIONS.	Mean Tide.	Ocean Level.	
Lebanon Junction (*a*).......LVII	444	447	
Cumberland Street..............	425	428	
Plank Road.....................	438	441	
Killian's Road.................	534	537	
Coleman's Road.................	534	537	
Furnace Run....................	539	542	
Cornwall (*b*).................	576	579	

a Junction with Lebanon Valley R. R. near Lebanon.
b Opposite the Middle of the Ore Hill.

LXI. East Penn R. R.

STATIONS.	Mean Tide.	Ocean Level.	
Reading (*a*)..................L	(264)	(267)	
Temple.........................			
Blandon........................	405	408	
Fleetwood......................			
Lyons..........................	460	463	
Bower's........................			
Topton Junction (*b*)..........	471	474	
Mertztown......................			
Shamrock.......................			
Alburtis Intersection (*c*)......LV	427	430	
Millerstown....................			
Emaus Station (*d*)...........LIV	417	420	
Penn Junction (*e*)............	260	263	
Allentown......................			

a Reading R. R.
b Branch R. R. to Kutztown.
c Fogelsville R. R.—Colebrookdale R. R.
d Perkiomen R. R.
e Lehigh Valley R. R., just below Allentown, where the 260 (263) elevation is supposed to apply.

LXII. Little Schuylkill R. R.

STATIONS.	Mean Tide.	Ocean Level.	
Port Clinton (*a*)..............L	(397)	(400)	
Drehersville...................			
Ringgold.......................	541	544	
Hecla..........................			
Reynolds.......................			
Tamaqua (*b*)..................	787	790	

a Reading R. R.
b South side of Broad Street.—Mountain Link and Schuylkill Valley R. R. —East Mahanoy R. R.

LXIII. *Schuylkill and Susquehanna R. R.*

STATIONS.	Mean Tide.	Ocean Level.	
Auburn Junction (*a*)..........L	(457)	(460)	
Jefferson......................			
Summit........................			
White Horse....................			
Stanhope......................			
Pinegrove Junction.............	511	514	
L. & P. R. R. Junction (*b*)..LIX	(491)	(494)	
Ellwood.......................			
Gold Mine.....................			
Rausch Gap....................			
Cold Spring...................			
Yellow Spring.................			
Rattling Run..................			
Forge.........................			
Dauphin (*c*)..................			
Rockville (*d*)..................I	(343)	(350)	

a Reading R. R.
b Lebanon and Pinegrove R. R., or Lebanon and Tremont.
c East side of the Susquehanna River.
d East side of Susquehanna River, crossing Pennsylvania R. R. at grade, at the east end of the long bridge, 5 miles above Harrisburg.

LXIV. *Mine Hill and Schuylkill Haven R. R.*

STATIONS.	Mean Tide.	Ocean Level.	
Schuylkill Haven (*a*)..........L	(520)	(523)	
Westwood Junction	654	657	
Summit........................	860	863	
Tremont.......................	758	761	
Westwood Junction, as above....	(654)	(657)	
Minersville...................	684	687	
Mine Hill Gap.................	816	819	
Glen Carbon...................	1136	1139	
Head of Mine Hill Plane, No. 1 ..	1519	1522	
Foot of Gordon Plane...........	773	776	
Centralia.................CXV	1465	1468	
Potts Colliery, Locust Dale......	1095	1098	

a Junction with Philadelphia and Reading R. R.

LXV. Catawissa and Williamsport R. R.

STATIONS.	Mean Tide.	Ocean Level.	
Tamaqua (*a*)............LXVIII	(787)	(790)	
East Mahanoy Junction (*b*)......	(1093)	(1096)	
Tamenend (*c*)..................	1291	1294	
Quakeake Junction (*d*)......CXV	1350	1353	
Summit	1542	1545	
Girard.........................			
Girard Passing.................			
Brandonville....................			
Ringtown	1332	1335	
Beaver.........................			
McAuley	759	762	
Mainville......................	674	677	
D. W. & H. R. R. (*e*)......CXVI	476	479	
Catawissa	474	477	
North Branch (*f*)..............	481	484	
Rupert (*g*)			
Danville.......................	493	496	
Mooresburg....................			
Pottsgrove......................	494	497	
Dougal	501	504	
Milton.........................			
P. & E. R. R. Crossing (*h*) CCXIII	480	483	
Datesman's....................			
West Branch (*i*)...............	475	478	
New Columbia..................			
White Deer....................	486	489	
Allenwood.......			
Fritz...........................			
Montgomery			
P. & E. R. R. Crossing (*j*) CCXIII	500	503	
Susquehanna River (*k*)..........	505	508	
Muncy	504	507	
Hall's..........................	521	524	
Montoursville..................	534	537	
Loyalsock Creek (*l*)	535	538	
P. & E.R.R. Crossing (*m*) CCXIII	542	545	
Williamsport Depot (*n*).........	530	533	

a b East Mahanoy R. R.

c Junction with Lehigh and Susquehanna Division of Central R. R. of N. J.

d With Lehigh Valley R. R.

e Crossing Danville, Hazelton and Wilkesbarre R. R. below Catawissa.

f Susquehanna River, water 29′ below rail.

g Junction with Lackawanna and Bloomsburg R. R.

h Crossing P. & E. R. R. (Milton).

i Susquehanna River, West Branch, water 28′ below rail.

j Crossing P. & E. R. R. (Montgomery).

k Water 30′ below rail.

l Water 13′ below rail.

m Crossing P. & E. R. R. (Williamsport).

n The level of the Philadelphia and Erie R. R. at this point is given in Table CCXIII, as 510.43 feet above Ocean Level.

LXVI. *Mill Creek R. R.*

STATIONS.	Mean Tide.	Ocean Level.	
Pottsville (*a*)....................L	(603)	(606)	
Mount Carbon (*a*)...............L	(591)	(594)	
Mill Creek Junction..............	622	625	
Port Carbon (*b*)..........LXVII	627	630	
Dormer's			
St. Clair..........................			
Lanigan Furnace................	706	709	
John's Mines.....................	827	830	
New Castle.......................	875	878	
Head of Grade....................			
Frackville.........................			

a a Philadelphia and Reading R. R.
b Junction with Schuylkill Valley R. R.

LXVII. *Schuylkill Valley R. R.*

STATIONS.	Mean Tide.	Ocean Level.	
Pottsville (*a*)....................L			
Mt. Carbon (*a*)..................L			
Port Carbon (*b*)...........LXVI			
Eagle Hill.........................			
Cumbola............................			
New Philadelphia			
Middleport.........................	712	715	
Brockville..........................			
Tuscarora..........................	895	898	
Newkirk.............................			
Tamaqua (*c*)................LXII	(787)	(790)	

a a Philadelphia and Reading R. R.
b Junction with Mill Creek R. R.
c Junction with Little Schuylkill R. R.

LXVIII. *East Mahanoy R. R.*

STATIONS.	Mean Tide.	Ocean Level.	
Tamaqua (*a*)........LXII, LXV	(787)	(790)	
East Mahanoy Junction.... LXV	1093	1096	
" " Tunnel, south end	1312	1315	
" " " north end	1334	1337	
Mahanoy City Depot........CXV	1235	1238	

a End of Little Schuylkill R. R. Catawissa and Williamsport R. R.

LXIX. *Mahanoy and Shamokin R. R.*

STATIONS.	Mean Tide.	Ocean Level.	
Head of Grade (*a*)	1472	1475	
Head of Mahanoy Plane	1479	1482	
Foot of Mahanoy Plane	1127	1130	
St. Nicholas Colliery	1155	1158	
New Boston Colliery	1520	1523	
Ashland Depot	881	884	
Summit	1155	1158	
Keystone	1025	1028	
Benjamin Franklin Colliery	1175	1178	
Locust Summit	1238	1241	
Monteliers Colliery	1072	1075	
Coal Ridge Colliery, No. 2	1131	1134	
Preston Colliery, No. 1	1090	1093	
Cuyler Colliery, Raven Run	1360	1363	
Girardville	1051	1054	
Shenandoah City Depot	1244	1247	
Head of Big Mine Run Plane	1275	1278	
Locust Gap Junction	1029	1032	
Greenback Colliery	895	898	
Shamokin Depot	730	733	
Trevorton Colliery	760	763	
Herndon Junction (*b*)	423	426	

a South side Broad Mountain Summit.
b Junction with Northern Central R. W. at Herndon Station, 13½ miles from Trevorton.

NOTE. There are scores of small branching colliery roads and tracks to coal mines not mentioned in the foregoing tables. Civil and mining engineers in the Coal Region are earnestly requested to furnish all the authentic levels of the intersections of such roads, levels of switches, levels of mouths of gangways, and levels of determinate recognizable points on the surface, high and low, in their possession, to make this portion of the hypsometrical records of Pennsylvania as complete and useful as possible. [J. P. L.]

LXX. *Schuylkill Canal.*

The elevations on the Schuylkill Canal, were copied from a list furnished by Mr. James F. Smith, Chief Engineer, Reading, Penna.

The datum is mid tide, Philadelphia. The levels are deduced from a survey made in 1846.

Schuylkill Navigation Company. Elevation of Combs of Dams.

NAMES OF DAM.	No.	Above Mid-Tide.	Ocean Level.	Name of Town.
Fairmount	32	10	13	
Flatrock	31	36.10	39	
Plymouth	30	45.87	49	Conshohocken.
Norristown	29	57.36	60	
Catfish	28	62.19	65	
Pawlings	27	66.49	69	Perkiomen.
Black Rock	26	84.61	88	Phœnixville.
Vincent	25	102.07	105	
Lewis	24	177.86	181	
Poplar Neck	23	184.88	188	Lower Reading.
Kissingers	22	204.38	207	
Shepps	21	213.09	216	
Leizes	20	221.46	224	
Felix's	19	236.27	240	
Herbine's	18	265.95	269	Leesport.
Kernsville	17	364.93	368	
Blue M'tn.	16	389.83	393	
Hummels	15	409.03	412	
Lords	14	432.98	436	
Cross Cut	13	443.93	447	Auburn.
Dam No.	12	451.23	454	
" "	11	471.53	475	
" "	10	476.93	480	
" "	9	483.33	486	
" "	8	490.63	494	
" "	7	509.23	512	Schuylkill Haven.
" "	6	551.38	554	
" "	5	574.36	577	Second Mountain.
" "	4	583.83	587	Mount Carbon.
" "	3	592.23	595	" "
" "	2	613.83	617	Palo Alto.
" "	1	618.63	622	Port Carbon.

NOTE.—Levels as taken from a profile in the Penna. Canal Co'.s Office, at Harrisburg, made under the direction of J. Dutton Steele, Civil Engineer, in 1851.

TOWNS.	Above Tide.		
Mount Carbon	620		
Schuylkill Haven	511		
Port Clinton	392		
Reading	195		
Pottstown	147		
Norristown	49		

LXXI. Union Canal.

The elevations on the Union Canal, were copied from a statement, giving number and lifts of locks, furnished through the kindness of Mr. B. B. Lehman, of Lebanon, Pa., formerly Chief Engineer and Genral Superintendent of the Union Canal.

Elevation of Locks on Union Canal from Lebanon, Eastward.

NO. OF LOCK.	Above Tide.	Ocean Level.	
Lock No. 1	475.50		
" 2	471		
" 3	466.50		
" 4	462		
" 5	457.50		
" 6	453		
" 7	447.50		
" 8	440.50		
" 9	433.50		
" 10	427.50		
" 11	421.50		
" 12	414.50		
" 13	407.50		
" 14	401.50		
" 15	395.50		
" 16	387.50		
" 17	379.50		
" 18	373.50		
" 19	368.50		
" 20	362.50		
" 21	356.50		
" 22	351.50		
" 23	346.50		
" 24	340.50		
" 25	334.50		
" 26	328.50		
" 27	322		
" 28	315.50		
" 29	310.50		
" 30	305.50		
" 31	300.50		
" 32	295.50		
" 33	290.50		
" 34	285.50		
" 35	280.50		
" 36	275.50		
" 37	269.50		
" 38	264.50		
" 39	258.50		
" 40	253.50		
" 41	247.50		
" 42	241.50		
" 43	235.50		
" 44	230.50		
" 45	225.50		
" 46	220.50		
" 47	215.50		
" 48	210.50		
" 49	205.50		
" 50	200.50		
" 51	192.50		
" 52	185.50		
" 53	179		
" 54	169		

Lebanon (or Summit Level Union Canal) 480
Middletown (Mouth of Swatara Creek) 266
Reading (Schuylkill River) 169
Pinegrove (Basin at former head of Navigation) 483½

Elevation of Locks on Union Canal from Lebanon, Westward.

NO. OF LOCK.	Above Tide.	Ocean Level.	
Lock No, 1	474.60		
" 2	469.20		
" 3	463.80		
" 4	458.40		
" 5	453		
" 6	447.60		
" 7	442.20		
" 8	436.80		
" 9	431.40		
" 10	426		
" 11	420.60		
" 12	415.20		
" 13	409.80		
" 14	404.40		
" 15	399		
" 16	393.60		
" 17	384.60		
" 18	376.60		
" 19	368.60		
" 20	362.60		
" 21	356.60		
" 22	351.10		
" 23	345.60		
" 24	340.10		
" 25	334.60		
" 26	329.60		
" 27	324.60		
" 28	319.60		
" 29	314.60		
" 30	309.60		
" 31	303.60		
" 32	297.60		
" 33	291.60		
" 34 (At Middletown)	285.60		
Susquehanna River / Mouth of Swatara Creek	266		

LXXII. Lebanon Valley R. R. (Steele.)

Note.—This list was copied from a profile in the office of the Pennsylvania Company, at Harrisburg, made under the direction of J. Dutton Steele, Civil Engineer, in 1857.

STATIONS.	Above Tide.	Ocean Level.	
Harrisburg I	314		
Hummelstown...................	362		
Palmyra	442		
Annville.........................	395		
Lebanon	460		
Myerstown	468		
Womelsdorf	440		
Reading	253		
Birdsboro	165		
Pottstown.......................	137		
Phœnixville.....................	97		
Norristown......................	58		
Manayunk Falls................	51		

III. LEHIGH SERIES.

C. *North Pennsylvania R R*

The levels on the North Pennsylvania R. R. were copied from the profile in the office of the Company, by permission of Mr. S. W. Roberts, Chief Engineer and General Superintendent.

The datum, or base of levels, is Philadelphia City datum, 8.733′ above mean surface of Atlantic Ocean. *Therefore 9 feet is added to make the second column.*

STATIONS.	City Datum.	Ocean Level.	
Philadelphia Depot (*a*)..........	19	28	
Cohocksink	25	34	
Diamond Street..................	30	39	
Somerset Street..................	69	78	
P. & R. Coal R. R. Crossing (*b*). .L	70	79	
Tioga Street	94	103	
Frankford Lane...................	92	101	
Fisher's Lane.....................	110	119	
Green Lane........................	156	165	
Oak Lane..........................	192	201	
City Line..........................	184	193	
York Road........................	176	185	
Chelton Hills.....................	181	190	
Paxon's Road.....................	225	234	
Abingdon Junction (*c*)........CII	245	254	
Edge Hill..........................	284	293	
Camp Hill.........................	169	178	
Edgehillville Road...............	167	176	
Fort Washington.................	161	170	
Ambler............................	190	199	
Pennllyn.	230	239	
Gwynedd..........................	262	271	

a At Willow Street.
b Crossing Philadelphia & Reading R. R.
c Intersection of Northeast Pennsylvania R. R. at Abington.

STATIONS.	City Datum.	Ocean Level.
Wissahickon Creek..............	342	351
Lansdale Junc. (*d*).....CIII, CIV	359	368
Hatfield........................	302	311
Zetty's Road....................	339	348
Nigger Hill.....................	443	452
Sellersville....................	322	331
Tunnel..........................	444	453
Koffler's Gap...................	521	530
Bunker Hill.....................	519	528
Quakertown......................	487	496
Hilltop.........................	546	555
Coopersburg.....................	540	549
Summit (*e*)....................	591	600
Koch's Mill.....................	364	373
Yeager's Mill...................	339	348
Wagner's Mill...................	279	288
Hellertown......................	267	276
Hampton.........................	267	276
Shimersville R.R. (*f*)........CV	255	264
Hess' Mill......................	259	268
Zinc Works......................	238	247
Bethlehem (*g*).................	228	237

A profile in the office of the Pennsylvania Canal Company, at Harrisburg, made under the direction of J. Dutton Steele, Civil Engineer, in 1857, gives the following very different levels of some of the points mentioned in the above list, and of others not mentioned in it. Some of the names seem to have been altered or reversed:

Wingohocking (Frankford Lane?) 92; Fisher's Lane, 110; City Lane (Oak Lane?) 192; Edgehill (York Road?) 175; Edgehill, 284; Fort Washington, 158; Wissahickon (Ambler?) 190; Gwynedd, 229! North Wales, 377; Lansdale, 371; Nigger-Hill, 440; Sellersville, 311; Koffler's Gap, 524; Bunker Hill, 519; Quakertown, 489; Same's Gap, 597; Hellertown, 270; Bethlehem, 249.

The datum is "Tide."

CI. Delaware and Bound Brook R. R.

NOTE. For this road which is virtually a branch of the North Pennsylvania, leaving it at Jenkintown Station. See Appendix.
For the *Philadelphia and Newtown R. R.*, see under CLIII.

d Doylestown Branch and Stony Creek R. R. Crosses at Lansdale.

e Highest Point noted on profile of North Pennsylvania R. R. end of section 44, near Coopersburg, 591.50.

f Point of divergence of Shimersville Branch.

g The North Pennsylvania R. R. intersects the Lehigh Valley R. R. at this point.

CII. Northeast Pennsylvania R. R.

The levels on the Northeast Pennsylvania R. R. were furnished by Mr. S. W. Roberts, Chief Engineer and General Superintendent, N. P. R. R.

Base of levels, Philadelphia City datum, 8.733 above Ocean Level. Therefore nine feet is added to make second column.

STATIONS.	City Datum.	Ocean Level.	
Abington Junction (*a*)..........C	250	259	
Summit..........................	333	342	
Willow Grove..................	250	259	
Heaton..........................			
Pennepack Creek...............	160	169	
Fulmore..........................			
Hatsborough....................	220	229	
Hartsville.......................	233	242	

a Junction with the North Pennsylvania R. R. near Abington.

CIII. Doylestown Branch N. P. R. R.

The elevations on the Doylestown Branch of the North Penn R. R. were furnished by Mr. S. W. Roberts, Chief Engineer.

Base of levels, Philadelphia City datum, 8.733 above Ocean Level.

STATIONS.	City Datum.	Ocean Level.	
Lansdale Junction (*a*)..........C	359	368	
Temperance Road...............	350	359	
Neshaminy Creek...............	260	269	
Road to Lexington.............	242	251	
Cooke's Run....................	242	251	
Bristol Road....................	294	303	
Doylestown (*b*).................	338	347	

a Point of divergence from N. P. R. R. at, or near Lansdale.
b Depot Ground at Doylestown.

CIV. Stony Creek R. R.

The levels on Stony Creek R. R. were copied from a profile furnished through the kindness of Mr. A. R. Roberts, Assistant Engineer, N. P. R. R.

The datum was fixed on the assumption that the elevation of the water in the Schuylkill River pool *below* Norristown, stood 49′ above Mean Tide at Philadelphia. The elevation of the comb of the dam *at* Norristown, as shown by the notes of the Schuylkill Navigation Company, at Reading, Pa., is 57.36′ above mid tide at Philadelphia.

The third column is made by adding three feet (3.349) to reduce to Mean Tide at Philadelphia to Ocean Level.

STATIONS.	Above Assumed Datum.	Mean Tide.	Ocean Level.	
Lansdale Junc. (*a*)....C	*350	†359	362	
1st Mile Post...........	350	359	362	
2d Mile Post............	330	339	342	
Summit (*b*).......	350	359	362	
1st Crossing of Stony Cr.	215	224	227	
2d Crossing of Stony Cr.	142	151	154	
3d Crossing of Stony Cr.	104	113	116	
Norristown (*c*).......LI	50	59	62	

a With North Penn R. R. and with Doylestown Branch R. R.

* Elevation as shown on profile.

† Elevation of Railroad Crossing as shown on profile of North Penn. R. R. Levels at the other stations of the table are made to correspond with the level of North Penn R. R., by adding 9 feet to Mr. Roberts' original figures.

b Between Wissahickon and Stony Creek.

c The level given in Table LI, of the Philadelphia and Reading R. R., Germantown and Norristown Branch, at Norristown is 62 (65 Ocean Level).

CV. Shimersville Branch N. P. R. R.

STATIONS.	Above Tide.	Ocean Level.	
Junction (*a*)...................C	255	258	
Junction (*b*) CXIV	217	220	

a Point of divergence from N. P. R. R. near Bethlehem.

b Junction with Lehigh Valley R. R.

CVII. Lehigh and Susquehanna R. R.

NOTE.—This road runs on the north and east bank of the Lehigh River most of the way. Its levels are similar to those of the Lehigh Valley road on the opposite bank.

STATIONS.	Tide.	Ocean Level.	
Easton (*a*).....................			
Freemansburg..................			
Bethlehem (*b*)............CXIII	(240)	(243)	
Allentown Station...............			
Catasauqua (*c*)			
Laubach's.......................			
Siegfried's Bridge			
Treichler's.....................			
Walnut Port....................			
Lehigh Gap			

a Junction with Morris & Essex R. R.

b Junction with N. Penna. and with Lehigh and Lackawanna R. R's.

c Junction with Cat. & Fogelsville R. R.

STATIONS.	Tide.	Ocean Level.	
Parryville			
Weissport			
Lehighton			
Mauch Chunk (*d*)			
Penn Haven Junction			
Rockport			
White Haven (*e*)			
Penobscot			
Ashley (*f*)			
Wilkesbarre			
Pittston			
Moosic			
Scranton (*g*)			
Green Ridge (*h*)			

CVIII. Mauch Chunk and Switch Back R. R.

Mauch Chunk			
Summit Hill			

CIX. Nesquehoning Valley R. R.

Mauch Chunk			
Nesquehoning			
Hauto			
Hometown			
Tamenend			

CX. Tamaqua Branch R. R.

Hauto			
Coledale			
Tamaqua			

CXI. Nescopec Branch R. R.

White Haven			
Upper Lehigh			

CXII. Nanticoke Branch R. R.

Ashley			
Sugar Notch			
Hanover			
Nanticoke			
Wanamie			

d Junction with Nesquehoning Valley Branch; M. C. Summit Hill and Switchback R. R.

e Junction with Nescopec Branch.

f Junction with Nanticoke Branch.

g Junction with Del. Lack. & Western R. R.

h Junction with Delaware & Hudson R. R.

CXIII. *Lehigh and Lackawanna R. R.*

The elevations on the Lehigh and Lackawanna R. R., were furnished by Mr. Charles Brodhead, President of the Company, who says, "Our surveys carry us into the *Wind Gap;* and the highest point on the Turnpike, *in the Gap*, we found to be 738 feet above Bethlehem, or 978 feet above tide." The road runs as far as Steuben, 15 miles.

STATIONS.	Mean Tide.	Ocean Level.	
Bethlehem Junction (*a*)....CVII	240	243	
Peter's Mills....................	255	258	
Shimer's.........................	287	290	
Reiter...........................			
Brodhead	315	318	
Steuben	333	336	
Bath	401	404	
Chapman..........................	576	579	

a With Lehigh and Susquehanna R. R. at Bethlehem, on the north side of the Lehigh River.

CXIV. *Lehigh Valley R. R.*

The levels on the Lehigh Valley R. R. were copied from a list furnished by Mr. Robert H. Sayre, Chief Engineer and General Superintendent, Lehigh Valley R. R.

The datum is Mean Tide, Delaware River, three feet being added for Ocean Level in the second column.

Note on the Lehigh Canal Levels.

By a printed list of levels in the possession of Mr. George Ruddle, of Mauch Chunk, it appears that there is a rise in the

Lower grand section of Slackwater Navigation, from the Delaware River to Mauch Chunk (46 miles), of..................	360′.87
Upper grand section, Mauch Chunk to Wright's Creek (26 miles), of.	599′.83
Upper grand section, Wright's Creek to Stoddart's Ville (miles), of..............................	336′.00
Adding to these figures, for the height of Bixler's Rift, Delaware Canal, above low tide in Delaware River.................	160.40
we get the following heights of the Lehigh Slackwater System:	
At Mauch Chunk, 360.87 + 160.40 = ...	521.23
At Wright's Creek, 521.23 + 599.83 = ...	1121.10
At Stoddart's Ville, 1121.10 + 336 = ...	1457.10

STATIONS.	Mean Tide.	Ocean Level.	
Philipsburg (*a*).............CL	208	211	
Delaware River, here............	(148)	(151)	
Easton	202	205	
Redington.......................			
Freemansburg....................	219	222	

a 60′ above Delaware River, Junction with Central R. R. of N. J., Morris and Essex R. R., Belvidere and Delaware R. R.

STATIONS.	Mean Tide.	Ocean Level.
Bethlehem....................	231	234
North Penn R. R. Junction (*b*).C	247	250
East Penn R. R. Junction...LXI		
Allentown....................	251	254
Catasauqua...............CXV	277	280
Hokindauqua............CXV *bis*		
Whitehall....................	297	300
Coplay.......................		
Laury's......................	326	329
Slatington...................	363	366
Lehigh Gap...................	385	388
Lehighton....................	461	464
Mauch Chunk (*c*)..........CVIII	553	556
Glen Onoko...................		
Penn Haven Junction......CXVI	705	708
Hickory Run..................		
Rockport (*d*).................	910	913
White Haven..................	1150	1153
Summit (*e*)..................	1742	1745
Fairview (*f*).................	1675	1678
Newport......................	1024	1027
Warrior Run..................	710	713
Sugar Notch..................	670	673
South Wilkesbarre............	550	553
Wilkesbarre (*g*)..............	553	556
Plainsville..................	550	553
Pittston...............CXVIII	572	575
Lackawanna Junction (*h*)....CLV	572	575
Ransom.......................	584	587
Falls	590	593
McKunes'.....................	600	603
Lagrange.....................	600	603
Tunkhannock.............CXIX	614	617
Vosburg......................	617	620
Mehoopany	636	639
Meshoppen (*i*)................	646	649
Black Walnut.................	653	656
Laceyville...................	663	666
Wyalusing....................	678	681
Frenchtown	694	697
Rumnerfield..................	700	703
Standing Stone...............	706	709
Wysauking	716	719
Towanda (*j*)..............CXX	738	741
Ulster.......................	743	746
Athen's Bridge...............	776	779
Waverly (*k*).............CLXII	823	826

b Junction with East Penn. R. R. Elevation given by Philadelphia and Reading R. R. at this point 260′.
c 40′ above Lehigh River.
d 35′ above Lehigh River.
e Nescopeck Mountain.
f Top of Wyoming Mountain.
g 30′ above Susquehanna River.
h 35′ above Susquehanna River, Junction with Delaware, Lackawanna and Western R. R.
i 35′ above Susquehanna River at Meshoppen.
j 28′ above Susquehanna River at Towanda.
k 25′ above Chemung River. At Waverly joins the New York and Erie R. R.

CXV. *Catasauqua and Fogelsville R. R.*

The levels of the Catasauqua and Fogelsville R. R. were furnished through the courtesy of Mr. Joshua Hunt, President of the Company.

The datum is Lehigh Valley R. R. at Catasauqua; which is 277′ above tide; and therefore 280′ above Ocean Level, as shown in the second column.

STATIONS.	Above Catasauqua.	Ocean Level.
Catasauqua	0	280
Seiple's	183	463
Jordan Bridge (*a*)	165	445
Guth's	209	489
Walbert	268	548
Chapman	259	539
Trexlertown (*b*)	129	409
Spring Creek	101	381
Alburtis (*c*)	173	453
Lock Ridge	158	438
Gardner	387	667
Red Lion	511	791
Rittenhouse Gap	658	938

a Water in creek at Jordan Bridge, 81 feet = Catasauqua; 361′ = Tide.
b Allentown R. R. Crossing on grade.
c East Pennsylvania R. R. Crossing.

CXV *bis.* *Trenton R. R.*

NOTE. No levels of this road could be obtained.

CXVI. *Lehigh Valley Coal Branches.*

The elevations on the Branch Railroads owned by the Lehigh Valley R. R. Company were furnished by Mr. Robert H. Sayre, Chief Engineer and General Superintendent.

The datum is mean Tide, Delaware River.

STATIONS.	Mean Tide.	Ocean Level.
Penn Haven Junction (*a*)	705	708
Black Creek (*b*)	1015	1018
Weatherly	1090	1093
Hazle Creek Junction (*c*)	1325	1328
Hazleton		
Eckley		
Hazel Creek Junction (*c*)	1325	1328
Beaver Meadow	1355	1358
Lewiston		
Jeanesville	1680	1683
Yorktown Crossing (*d*)	1750	1753

a With Lehigh Valley R. R.
b Leaves here the Quakeake R. R. or Mahanoy Division.
c Of the Beaver Meadow R. R. with the Hazleton R. R.
d Divide between the Lehigh and Susquehanna waters.

STATIONS.	Mean Tide.	Ocean Level.	
Audenreid......................	1735	1738	
Hartz's........................			
Quakake Junction (*e*)	1315	1318	
Delano (*f*)....................	1665	1668	
Mahanoy City Junction.....LXV	1552	1555	
Mahanoy City...........LXVIII	1230	1233	
Shenandoah	1268	1271	
Raven Run			
Centralia (*g*).............LXIV	1484	1487	
Mount Carmel..................	1056	1059	
Locust Gap.....................	1027	1030	
Fulton	960	963	
Shamokin (*h*)..................	730	733	
Zerbe Summit (*i*)................	1073	1076	
Zerbe Colliery.................	905	908	

e Crosses at Yorktown the Catawissa R. R. Elevation (as given by Philadelphia and Reading R. R. at this point) 1350′ feet above tide!

f Delano is on the divide between Schuylkill and Susquehanna waters.

g Centralia is on the divide between the Mahanoy and Shamokin waters.

h Shamokin Station 70′ above the town.

i Zerbe Summit divides the Shamokin and Little Mahanoy waters.

CXVII. Danville, Hazleton and Wilkesbarre R. R.

The elevations on the Danville, Hazleton and Wilkesbarre R. R. were furnished by Mr. A. B. Starr, Assistant Engineer, P. & E. R. R.

The datum is *high* tide at the Schuylkill River, at Philadelphia. Add seven feet for Ocean Level.

STATIONS.	High Tide.	Ocean Level.	
Sunbury Junction (*a*)	436	443	
Kline's Grove..................	438	445	
Wolverton......................	435	442	
Kipp's Run.....................	456	463	
Danville (*b*).....................	456	463	
Roaring Creek..................	452	459	
Catawissa	464	471	
R. R. Crossing (*c*)...............	463	470	
Mainville......................	582	589	
Mifflin Cross Roads............	804	811	
Scotch Valley..................	1008	1017	
Summit	1030	1037	
Wolfton........................	1016	1023	
Rock Glen......................	914	921	
Gowan..........................	992	999	
Tomhicken (*d*)..................	1221	1228	

a Shamokin R. R. with Northern Central R. R. at Sunbury.

b With Lackawanna and Bloomsburg R. R.

c Catawissa R. R. Crossing; Elevation of Catawissa R. R. at same point 476.

d With Lehigh Valley R. R.

CXVIII. Pennsylvania Coal Company's R. R.

Elevations on the Pennsylvania Coal Company's R. R. from Pittston (or Port Griffith) to Hawley were copied from a profile in the Company's office at Pittston, Pa., by permission of Mr. George Johnson, Engineer.

The datum is 0 at foot of Plane No. I = 567.'28 above Sea Level.

	STATIONS.	Profile.	Above Tide.
Loaded track going out from Pittston.	Head of Plane..........No. 1	108	675
	" " .... " 2	206	773
	" " .... " 3	246	813
	" " .... " 4	397	964
	" " .... " 5	495	1062
	" " (Dunmore) " 6	550	1117
	" " .... " 7	697	1274
	" " .... " 8	888	1455
	" " .... " 9	1077	1644
	" " .... " 10	1255	1822
	" " .... " 11	1217	1784
	Tunnel	1400	1967
	Base of Plane............No. 12	779	1346
	Head of Plane............No. 12	928	1495
	Hamlin	329	896
Empty track back to Port Griffith's.	Head of Plane..........No. 13	511	1078
	" " .... " 14	640	1207
	" " .... " 15	733	1300
	" " .... " 16	830	1397
	" " .... " 17	874	1441
	" " .... " 18	955	1522
	" " .... " 19	998	1565
	" " .... " 20	952	1519
	" " .... " 21	1040	1607
	" " .... " 22	246	813
	Foot of Plane............ " 22	64	631

CXIX. Montrose R. W.

Elevations on the Montrose Railway were furnished by Mr. James I. Blakslee, President of the Company.

The datum, or base of levels, is that of grade on the Lehigh Valley R. R. at Tunkhannock.

STATIONS.	Mean Tide.	Ocean Level.
Tunkhannock (*a*)..........CXIV	614	617
Marcy..........................	968	971
Lemon..........................	1044	1047
Avery..........................	982	985
Meshoppen Creek..............	936	939
Lynn	1035	1038
Springville....................	1260	1263
Tylersville....................	1403	1406
Dimock	1510	1513
Hunter's.......................	1550	1553
Cool's.........................	1550	1553
Allenville	1652	1655
Montrose.......................	1659	1662

a Junction with Lehigh Valley R. R.

CXX. *Barclay and Schrader R. R.*

Elevations on the Barclay and Schrader R. R's were furnished by Mr. A. W. Stedman, Engineer of the Pa. & N. Y. R. R. & Coal Co., at Towanda, Pa., through the solicitation of Mr. James Macfarlane.

The datum is mean tide at Philadelphia.

STATIONS.	Mean Tide.	Ocean Level.	
Towanda (*a*)............CXIV	732	735	
Towanda (*b*)...	719	722	
Monroeton Junction (*c*)....CXXI	756	759	
Masontown (*d*)..................	788	792	
Greenwood.	817	820	
Lamoka..........................	1036	1039	
Foot of Plane (*e*)...............	1265	1268	
Head of Plane (*f*)	1750	1753	
Schrader R. R.*			
R. R. Switch (*g*)...............	1795	1798	
R. R. Switch (*h*)...............	1782	1785	
Carbon Run (*i*)..................	1923	1926	
Lowest Point (*j*)................	1970	1973	
Summit	2035	2038	

*This Railroad, four miles long, connects the Barclay R. R. with the Schrader Coal Mines.

a Switch at Upper Depot.
b Barclay Depot.
c With State Line and Erie R. R.
d Barclay R. R. Bridge rail.
e *Elevation estimated.*
f Rail in Plane-house.
g Upper Switch connecting with Barclay R. R.
h Lower Switch connecting with Barclay R. R.
i Rail under Breaker is 1923′.
j Lowest Point of Coal near Breaker.

CXXI. *State Line and Erie R. R.*

Levels on the State Line and Erie R. R. were copied from a profile in the office of the Company at Towanda, Bradford County, Pa. There were no stations, or names of towns, noted on the profile, the elevations being marked at mile posts, and therefore, the stations have been located from J. A. Anderson's R. R. map. The levels as shown in this list may not be entirely correct; but it is the only record which could be found.

The datum is Mean Tide at Philadelphia.

STATIONS.	Mean Tide.	Ocean Level.	
Monroeton Junction (*a*).....CXX	756	759	
Wilcox..........................	1117	1120	
New Albany......................	1191	1194	
Miller's	1324	1327	
Bushore.......................(?)	1587	1590	
Bernice	1852	1855	

a With Barclay R. R.

IV. DELAWARE SERIES.

CL. Philadelphia and Trenton R. R.

Levels on the Philadelphia and Trenton, and Belvidere Division of the Pennsylvania R. R. were furnished by Mr. F. B. Fiddler, Engineer in the office of the Company at Trenton, N. J. The levels were deduced from the original table of grades by Samuel H. Kneass, Engineer.

The datum of the Philadelphia and Trenton R. R. is mean tide at Philadelphia. The datum of the Belvidere Division of the Pennsylvania R. R. is water in canal at junction of feeder with Delaware and Raritan Canal near Trenton, which water level is four feet below the railroad track.

Philadelphia, Trenton and Belvidere Division, Pennsylvania R. R.

STATIONS.	Mean Tide.	Ocean Level.	
Philadelphia			
Kensington (*a*)	29	32	
Bridge over Frankford Creek	24	27	
Frankford Station (*b*)	29	32	
Bridesburg (*c*)	29	32	
Tacony	31	34	
Borics	32	35	
Cornwell's	36	39	
Eddington (*d*)	39	42	
Bristol (*e*)	18	21	
Tullytown	17	20	
Penn Valley	18	21	
Morrisville (*f*)	31	34	
Trenton Junction (*g*)	60	63	
Washington's Crossing	64	67	
Prime Hope Saw Mills	CLI		
Lambertville	72	75	
Prallsville	83	86	
Bull's Island (*h*)	94	97	
Warford's Rock	CLI		
Frenchtown	125	128	
Milford	137	140	
Holland	CLI		
Reigelsville	163	166	
Carpenterville	175	178	
Phillipsburg (*) ...CXIV	195	198	
Martin's Creek	231	234	
Belvidere	268	271	
Manunka Chunk	320	323	
Walker's Ferry Water Gap	CLI		

a Frankford Road Crossing.
b Middle of Church Street.
c Middle of Bridge Street.
d Dunk's Ferry Road.
e Middle of Market Street.
f N. E. side of Washington Street.
g The railroad track is four feet above the water in the canal.
h Elevation of railroad, head of Bull's Island, 97′. Low water in Delaware River 74′.

* Lehigh Valley R. R.

CLI. *Delaware River Levels.*

NOTE.—The following levels of ordinary low water in Delaware River above *mean tide at Philadelphia* (= 3.349 above mean ocean level) were obtained in the office of the Philadelphia and Trenton R. R. at Trenton, from Mr. F. B. Fiddler, C. E., deduced from the original grade tables by Mr. S. H. Kneass.

PLACES.	Mean Tide.	Ocean Level.
Trenton		
Washington's Crossing	20	23
Prime Hope Saw Mills	35	38
Lambertville	49	52
Bull's Island	71	74
Head of Bull's Island	74	77
Warford's Rock	91	94
Frenchtown	104	107
1.7 miles above " (*a*)	107.7	111
Milford	111	114
4 miles above " (*b*)	121.8	125
Holland	116	119
1½ miles below Reigelsville	124.2	127
Reigelsville	127	130
⅜ mile above "	130	133
1.6 mile above "	133.8	137
Carpenterville	137	140
2½ miles below Phillipsburg (*c*)	148.6	151
Phillipsburg	157	160
1¾ mile above "	165.2	168
2.7 miles above "	170.4	173
7.6 miles above "	192.8	196
2.84 miles above Martin's Cr. (*d*)	200.4	204
4.14 miles above "	210.9	214
Belvidere	232	235
Manunka Chunk	262	265
Walker's Ferry at Delaware Water Gap	298	301

CLII. *Delaware Canal.*

Elevations on the Delaware Canal were copied from a map made under the direction of the Lehigh Coal and Navigation Company, in 1826, by Isaac A. Chapman. The map is in possession of Mr. George Ruddle, Mauch Chunk.

The datum is low tide Delaware River, 3.349 above Ocean Level.

a Huntingdon County, N. J., 31.7 miles above Trenton.
b " " " not the Milford of Pike County, Pa.
c Opposite Easton, in New Jersey.
d Above Easton, in Pennsylvania.

POINTS ON LINE OF CANAL.	Low Tide.	
	Feet.	Inches
Trenton Falls; head; 49 miles below the mouth of Lehigh River	9	8
Gould's Rift; head	16	8
Yardleyville	18	
Scudder's Rift; head	24	8
Taylor's Rift; head	33	6
Buck Tail Rift; head	36	5
Will's Falls; head	49	9
New Hope	50	
33 miles below Lehigh River	53	3
Green Banks Rift; head	58	9
Gallopen's; head	68	3
Bull's Falls; head	72	2
26 miles below Lehigh River	72	9
Cut Bite Rift; head	77	4
Tumbling Dam Falls; head	89	1
Marshal's Island Rapids; head	100	7
Man of War Rift; head	102	3
Stunt's Falls; head	107	2
Firman's Falls; head	110	11
Nockamixon Falls; head	117	6
Linn's Falls; head	124	10
11 miles below Lehigh River	126	10
10 miles below Lehigh River	127	3
Durham Falls; head	130	3
9 miles below Lehigh River	130	4
Greavelly Falls; head	133	3
Rocky Falls; head	136	1
Ground Hog Rift; head	138	1
Old Sow Rift; head	145	7
Clifford's Rift; head	150	10
Bixler's Rift; head (*a*)	160	5

a This point is about one-half mile below the mouth of Lehigh River.

CLIII. Philadelphia and Newtown R. R.

NOTE.—See Appendix.

CLIV. Flemington R. R.

Levels on the Flemington R. R. were copied from a list prepared by Mr. F. B. Fiddler, in the R. R. office, at Trenton, N. J.

The datum is mean tide Delaware River, = 3.349 above Ocean Level.

STATIONS.	Mean Tide.	Ocean Level.	
Flemington Junction (*a*)......CL	73	76	
Mount Airy	147	150	
Ringoes	248	251	
Summit (*b*)	255	258	
Copper Hill	159	162	
Flemington	183	186	

a Junction with Belvidere and Delaware R. R.
b N. E. of Ringoes.

NOTE.—Two other short lists in New Jersey are here appended, on account of their connections with the Delaware River lines. Other New Jersey Railway levels are published by Prof. Cook in his Annual Reports of the Geological Survey of that State.

Morris and Essex R. R.

The Morris and Essex R. R. levels were furnished by Mr. James Archbald, Chief Engineer, Del. L. & W. R. R.

STATIONS.	Mean Tide.	Ocean Level.	
Phillipsburg.................CL	217	220	
Phalcony Creek................	341	344	
Stewartsville..................	370	373	
Washington Depot.............	503	506	
Port Murray....................	585	588	

Belvidere and Newtown R. R.

NOTE.—The Belvidere and Newtown levels were copied from a list furnished by Mr. F. B. Fiddler, Trenton, N. J.

STATIONS.	Mean Tide.	Ocean Level.	
R. R. Junction (*a*)...........CL	272	275	
Belvidere........................	283	286	
Sarepta..........................	361	364	
Hope	478	481	
Howell P. O....................	562	565	
Summit..........................	595	598	
Johnsburg.......................	568	571	
Summit	628	631	
Newton..........................	607	610	

a Junction with B. D. R. R.

CLV. Delaware, Lackawanna and Western R. R.

Elevations on the D. L. & W. R. R. were copied from a profile in the office of the Company at Scranton, by permission of the Assistant Engineer, Mr. Bryson.

The datum is mean tide, Delaware River, = 3.349 above Ocean Level.

STATIONS.	Above Tide.	Ocean Level.	Corrected.
Junction (Central R.R. of N. J)..			
Washington (Morris & Essex R.R.)			
Oxford Furnace................			
Bridgeville......................			
Manunka Chunk.............CL			
Delaware Bridge...............	290	293	
Portland.........................	288	291	
Delaware Water Gap..........	316	319	

STATIONS.	Above Tide.	Ocean Level.	Corrected.
Stroudsburg	400	403	
Spragueville	487	490	
*Henryville	593	596	
*Oakland	1008	1011	
*Paradise	1518	1521	
Forks			
Tobyhanna (*a*)	1929	1932	
Gouldsboro			
Summit	1887	1890	
*Moscow	1555	1558	
*Dunning's	1397	1400	
Greenville	1182	1185	
Scranton.........CLVI, CXVIII	740	743	
Clark's Summit	1239	1242	
Abington	1055	1058	
Factoryville	917	920	
Tunnel	963	966	
Nicholson	766	769	
Hopbottom	890	893	
Foster			
Oakley's	942	945	
Montrose Station	1050	1053	
New Milford	1084	1087	
Great Bend	876	879	
State Line	860	863	
Corbettsville	852	855	
Conklin	849	852	
Binghamton..............CLXII	843	846	

a The highest point noted on the profile, 1970 feet above tide. This point is between Tobyhanna & Summit.

* Elevations at stations marked thus (*) were not marked on the profile; neither could it be exactly determined what was the vertical scale of the profile; but it was supposed to be 290 feet to the inch.

The following list is therefore added, some of its figures corresponding exactly with those above. It was obtained from a profile in the office of the Pennsylvania Canal Co., at Harrisburg, made under the direction of J. Dutton Steele, in 1851.

STATIONS.	Above Tide.	Ocean Level.	
White House	170	173	
Lebanon	274	277	
Clinton	326	329	
New Hampton Summit	505	508	
West End Switch	498	501	
Delaware Bridge	293	296	
Delaware Water Gap	314	317	
Stroudsburg	422	425	
Naglesville	1961	1964	
Greenville	1182	1185	
Scranton	739	742	

CLVI. Bloomsburg Division, D. L. & W. R. R.

Elevations of the Bloomsburg Division of the Delaware, Lackawanna and Western R. R. were copied from notes, in the possession of Mr. A. Bryson, Jr., Div. Engineer, at Scranton, Pa. This list contains all the levels that could be obtained of this road.

STATIONS.	Mean Tide.	Ocean Level.	
Scranton CLV	740	743	
Taylorville......................	683	686	
Lackawanna Junction............	573	576	
Pittston..........................	573	576	
West Pittston....................	580	583	
Wyoming	560	563	
Maltby..........................	560	563	
Kingston........................	551	554	
Plymouth Junction..............	545	548	
Plymouth	539	542	
Avondale........................	534	537	
Nanticoke......................			
Hunlock's Creek................			
Schickshinny...................			
Beach Haven....................			
Berwick........................			
Brier Creek....................			
Espey..........................			
Bloomsburg			
Rupert....			
Catawissa Bridge...............			
Danville........................			
Northumberland................			
Sunbury........................			

CLVII. Lackawanna R. R.

Elevations on the Lackawanna R. R. between Carbondale and Scranton were furnished by Mr. A. H. Vaudling, Superintendent Delaware and Hudson Canal Co.'s R. R. at Providence, Luzerne County, Pa.

The datum is "Tide;" but whether high tide or mean tide is not known. Supposing it to be *mean* tide, 3.349 feet is added for Ocean Level.

STATIONS.	Above Tide.	Ocean Level.	
Carbondale (*a*)..............CLX	1083	1086	
Jermyn	968	971	
Archbald........................	965	968	
Olyphant........................	807	810	
Providence (*b*)................	700	703	

a Coal Brooke Breaker in Carbondale. The *canal level* at Carbondale is given by J. D. Steele as 965; see Table CLVIII.

b Elevation at the Lackawanna.

CLVIII. Carbondale & Honesdale R. R.

Levels on the Carbondale and Honesdale Railroad are in accordance with a profile furnished by Mr. A. H. Vandling, Superintendent of the Delaware and Hudson Canal Company, office of coal department, at Providence Penna. According to the profile which is marked, "Profile B, New Road," the *loaded* track starts from Carbondale at a point marked 1012 feet above tide; and the *empty* track starts at a point marked Honesdale 1000 feet above tide. In J. D. Steele's list (CLVIII) Carbondale and Honesdale are both alike called 965' above tide, at the level of the canal.

	STATIONS.	Above Carbondale.	Above Tide.	
Loaded cars, eastward.	Carbondale, lower end......	00	1012	
	Head of Plane 1............	240	1252	
	Head of Plane 2............	377	1389	
	Head of Plane 3............	579	1591	
	Head of Plane 4............	762	1774	
	Head of Plane 5 (*a*)	923	*1935	
	Head of Plane 6............	906	1918	
	Head of Plane 7............	572	1584	
	Foot of Plane 7 (*b*)..........	440	1452	
Empty cars back.	Honesdale........... CLIX	00	1000	1003
	Head of Plane 1............	180	1180	1183
	Head of Plane 2............	178	1178	1181
	Head of Plane 3............	290	1290	1293
	Head of Plane 4............	424	1424	1427
	Head of Plane 5............	502	1502	1505

CLIX. Honesdale Branch Erie Railway.

STATIONS.	Above Tide.	Ocean Level.	
Honesdale...............CLVIII	966		
White Mills....................	925		
Hawley	899		
Kimbles.........................	849		
Millville	780		
Rowlands	700		
Lackawaxen	650		

CLX. Delaware and Hudson Canal.

This list is from J. Dutton Steele's profile of 1851, in Penna. Canal Co'.s office, at Harrisburg.

TOWNS.	Above Tide.	Ocean Level.	
Carbondale...............CLVII	965		
Honesdale.......................	965		
Hawley..........................	880		
Port Jarvis.....................	455		
Port Clinton....................	455		

a Summit.
b From this point to Honesdale, a distance of 10 miles, there is a regular descent of 44 feet to the mile.

CLXI. Jefferson Branch, Erie Railway.

STATIONS.	Above Tide.	Ocean Level.	
Lanesboro Junction (*a*)....CLXII	982		
Ninevah Junction..............	981		
Brandts........................	1047		
Stevens Point..................	1078		
Webster's Mills................	1297		
Starrucca......................	1424		
Thompson.......................	1703		
Ararat Summit..................	2023		
Herrick Centre.................	1803		
Uniondale......................	1693		
Forrest City...................	1481		
Carbondale.....................	1079		

a With the Erie Railway at Lanesboro, in Susquehanna Co., Pa., about 190 miles from New York City. This road runs south to the Anthracite Coal field.

CLXII. Erie R. R. Line.

Levels on the Erie Railway were copied from profiles furnished by Mr. H. D. Blunden, Assistant Engineer. The profiles are complete, embracing the main line of road from Jersey City to Dunkirk, and all branches owned by the Erie Railway Company.

The datum is tide water at Jersey City. This, if *mean tide*, may be considered equivalent to Ocean Level.

Erie R. R.—Delaware Div.

STATIONS.	Above Tide.	Ocean Level.	
Port Jervis....................	440		
Pond Eddy......................	571		
Shoholo........................	648		
Lackawaxen................CLX	648		
Pine Grove.....................	668		
Narrowsburg....................	714		
Nobodys........................	748		
Cohecton.......................	748		
Callicoon......................	781		
Rock Run.......................	787		
Hawkins........................	809		
Basket.........................	830		
Bouchon........................	850		
Lordville......................	864		
Stockport......................	896		
Hancock........................	926		
Dickinsons.....................	954		
Hales Eddy.....................	974		
Deposit........................	1009		
Summit.........................	1373		
Susquehanna.............CLXI	914		

Erie R. R.—Susquehanna Div.

Great Bend	884		
Binghamton CLV	868		
Hooper	839		
Union	834		
Campville	830		
Owego	822		
Tioga	805		
Smithboro	799		
Waverly	836		
Chemung	820		
Wellsboro	831		
Elmira	863		
Corning CLXIV	942		
Painted Post	947		
Erwins	983		
Addison	993		
Rathboneville	1015		
Cameron Mills	1029		
Cameron	1056		
Santees	1067		
Adrian	1112		
Canesteo	1134		
Hornellsville	1161		

Erie R. R.—Western Div.

Tip Top Summit	1783		
Andover	1676		
Genessee	1511		
Scio	1458		
Philipsville	1390		
Belvidere	1384		
Friendship	1539		
Cuba Summit	1698		
Cuba	1542		
White House	1514		
Hindsdale	1501		
Olean	1438		
Allegheny	1422		
Vandalia	1415		
Carrollton CLXVI	1399		
Great Valley	1393		
Salamanca	1384		
Little Valley	1594		
Cattaraugus	1411		
Persia	1390		
Smith's Mills	1010		
Forestville	883		
Dunkirk (*a*)	600		

a The elevation given at Dunkirk by Lake Shore and Michigan Southern R. R., is 24.94 + 573. L. Erie = 597.94.

CLXIII. Erie R. R.—Buffalo Div.

STATIONS.	Above Tide.	Ocean Level.	
Arkport	1199		
Burns	1203		
Canesoraga	1260		
Garwoods	1280		
Swains	1312		
Turnout	1319		
Nunda	1336		
Hunts	1339		
Portage	1314		
Castile	1401		
Gainesville	1407		
Warsaw	1326		
Dale	1178		
Linden	1181		
Attica	998		
Tonawanda	1003		
Summit	1086		
Griswold	1044		
Darien	1024		
Alden	868		
Town Line	742		
Lancaster	683		
Checktowga	661		
East Buffalo	611		
Buffalo	588		

CLXIV. Corning, Cowanesque & Antrim Railway.

The levels on Corning, Cowanesque and Antrim Railway, were furnished by Mr. A. H. Gorton, Supt. The levels on this road have been reduced to the datum of the New York and Erie Railway, by adding 26 feet to Mr. Gorton's figures.

STATIONS.	Tide.	Corrected Tide.	
Corning CLXII	*918	†942	
Ernin Centre	952	976	
Lindley	973	997	
Lawrenceville CLXV	982	1006	
Nelson	1162	1186	
Elkland	1118	1142	
Lawrenceville CLXV	982	1006	
Tioga Village	1028	1052	
Holliday	1127	1151	
Middleburg	1154	1178	
Niles Valley	1168	1192	
Wellsboro	1295	1319	
Summit	1838	1862	
Antrim Coal Mines	1648	1672	

* Grade at Corning Junction according to Mr. Gorton.
† Grade at Corning Junction by profile of Erie Railway.

CLXV. Tioga R. R.

Levels on the Tioga R. R. were furnished by Mr. S. B. Elliott, Engineer of the T. R. R.

The datum is asserted to be that of the Erie R R. at Corning; in other words the following figures have been constructed on the basis of the Erie R. R. list, without reference to Mr. Gorton's intermediate station levels.

STATIONS.		Above Tide.	Ocean Level.
Lawrenceville CLXIV		1006	
Somer's Lane		1018	
Mitchell's Creek................		1022	
Old Station		1035	
Tioga..........................		1042	
Mill Creek		1077	
Lamb's Creek...................		1111	
Mansfield......................		1140	
Canoe Camp.....................		1163	
Covington......................		1208	
Blossburg......................		1348	
Morris Run (*a*).................		1678	
Arnot (*b*)......................		1682	
Fall Brook (*c*).................		1842	

a, *b*, *c* Coal Mines in the Blossburg Basin.

CLXVI. Bradford Branch, Erie Railway.

STATIONS.	Above Tide.	Ocean Level.	
Carrollton Junction (*a*)....CLXII	1400		
Ernins Mills	1409		
Limestone......................	1415		
Babcock	1429		
Bradford	1464		
DeGolias	1510		
Big Shanty	1715		
Crawfords	2098		
Summit (*b*).....................	2140		
Alton	2080		
Gilesville.....................	2016		

a With the Erie R. R., 407 miles from New York. This road runs south to the coal fields of McKean Co., Pa.

b Highest point on the profile just south of Crawfords.

V. SUSQUEHANNA SERIES.

CC. Northern Central.

Levels on the N. C. R. R. were copied from an old lithographed profile in the office at Baltimore, Md.

Datum: Mean tide at Baltimore; equivalent to + Ocean level.

STATIONS.	Mean Tide.	Ocean Level.	
Baltimore			
B. & P. R. R. Junction			
Mount Vernon	131		
Green Spring Junction (*a*) CCLV			
Timonium	381		
Cockeysville			
Sparks			
Monkton			
Parkton	420		
Freelands	596		
New Freedom	827		
Seitzland	611		
Glen Rock	551		
Hanover Junction (*b*)	422		
Smysers	389		
Glatfelter's	335		
Tunnel	299		
York (*c*) CCVI, CCVII	366		
Emigsville	376		
Mount Wolf	376		
Summit, No. 2	466		
Conewago Bridge	289		
York Haven	291		
Goldsboro	304		
Middletown Ferry	307		
Marsh Run	307		
New Cumberland	312		
Bridgeport (*d*) CCIX	355		
Marysville	350		
Dauphin (*e*) LXIII			
Clark's Ferry	361		
Halifax	378		
Liverpool			
Mohontongo			
Millersburg (*f*) CCXI	396		
Georgetown	417		
Trevorton Junction (*g*) LXIX	428		
Fisher's Ferry	433		
Selinsgrove	438		
Sunbury (*h*) CCXV	444		

a With Green Spring Branch N. C. R. R.

b With Hanover Branch, Han. & Gett. R. R.

c Junction with Peach Bottom R. R. and with York and Columbia R. R., and York & Gettysburg R. R.

d Opposite Harrisburg. Junction with Cumberland Valley R. R.

A list of levels of some of the above named points made by J. D. Steele, in 1851, was obtained in the office of the Penna. Canal Co., at Harrisburg, and is given for comparison, as follows:

STATIONS.	Mean Tide.	Ocean Tide.	
Mellvale	168		
Timonium	395		
Ashland	269		
Monckton	344		
Parkton	430		
Summit	860		
Glenrock	556		
Glatfelter's	472		
York	373		
Conewago Creek	285		
Bridgeport	343		
Dauphin	332		
Halifax	360		
Lykens V. R. R. Junction	380		
Millersburg	382		
Georgetown	417		
Sunbury CCXV	429		

CCI. Tide Water and Susquehanna Canal.

Levels on the T. W. & S. Canal, were copied from a profile in the office of the Schuylkill Navigation Company, at Reading, Pa., by permission of Mr. James F. Smith, Chief Engineer.

Datum, *low tide* at Havre de Grace. Information on the spot leads to the belief that the tide rises here 2½ feet.

Tide Water Canal.

STATIONS.	Above Low Tide.	Ocean Level.	
Level of Chesapeake Bay	0		
Lock No. 9, surface of water	10		
Lock No. 8, " "	16		
Lock No. 7, " "	26.5		
Lock No. 6, " "	37		
Lock No. 5, " "	47		
Lock No. 4, " "	57		
Lock No. 3, " "	67		
Lock No. 2, " "	77		

e Junction with Schuylkill and Susquehanna R. R.

f Junction with Lykens Valley Coal R. R. (Summit Branch R. R.)

g With Mahanoy and Shamokin Branch P. & Reading R. R.

h Junction 1. With Shamokin Division R. R. (CCXIV). 2. With Danville Hazleton and Wilkesbarre R. R. (CXVII). 3. With Philadelphia & Erie R. R. (CCXV). Note. The cars of the Northern Central run on the P. & E. R. R. to Williamsport, and then on the leased line from Williamsport to Canandaigua, once called the Williamsport and Elmira R. R., and now known as the northern extension of he Northern Central R. R.

Susquehanna Canal.

Lock No. 19, (next to No. 2, T. W. C)	85		
Lock No. 18, upper level........	93		
Lock No. 17, " "	103		
Lock No. 16, " "	114		
Lock No. 15, " "	123		
Lock No. 24, " "	125		
Lock No. 23, " "	134		
Lock No. 22, " "	143		
Lock No. 22, " "	152		
Lock No. 20, " "	161		
Lock No. 9, " "	170		
Lock No. 8, " "	177.5		
Lock No. 7, " "	185		
Lock No. 6, " "	193		
Lock No. 5, " "	201		
Lock No. 4, " "	209		
Lock No. 3, " "	217		
Lock No. 2, " "	225		
Lock No. 1, " "	233		
Aqueduct across Cabin Branch Creek......................	233		
Grand Lock at Wrightsville, opposite Columbia..............	233		

CCII. Pennsylvania Canal, E. D.

Elevations on the Pennsylvania Canal, Eastern Division, were furnished by Mr. Thos. T. Wierman, Jr.

Datum is *mean tide*, Chesapeake Bay.

STATIONS.	Mean Tide.		
Columbia Dam, surface..........	221		
Canal Basin, (Columbia).........	236		
Susquehanna River below Conewago Falls..................	244		
Susquehanna River above Conewago Falls..................	263		
Harrisburg Canal Basin (*a*)......	312		
Clark's Ferry Dam	333		

a Surface of water in the large (Porter's) Basin at Harrisburg 320

Floor of vestibule of the State Capital at Harrisburg 361

CCIII. Juniata Division Pennsylvania Canal.

Juniata River, Mouth :—			
Mitre Sill of Stop Lock at Junction.................. CCIV	347		
Millerstown dam, surface........	376		
Lewistown dam, "	442		
Canal at Lewistown "	450		
Anghwick dam, "	492		
Canal at Huntingdon "	586		
Huntingdon :			
Lower Mitre Sill of Lock No. 40	599		

CCIV. West Branch Division Pennsylvania Canal.

Juniata River, Mouth :—(*b*)			
Mitre Sill of Stop Lock at Junction..................CCIII	347		
Liverpool, water in River	368		
Liverpool, water in Canal	381		
Water in			
River below Shamokin dam ...	411		
Shamokin dam, at Sunbury....	419		
Canal at Northumberland..CCV	432		
Lewisburg dam (*c*)............	424		
Canal opposite Lewisburg......	445		
Muncy dam	459		
Loyalsoch dam and Canal......	502		
Canal at Williamsport	509		
Lock Haven dam..............	540		
Queens Run dam..............	546		
Bald Eagle dam...............	559		

b Surface of water of Pool of dam at Duncan's Island............332

c This dam has no connection with the Canal, and is therefore at a lower level.

CCV. Wyoming Division Pennsylvania Canal.

Northumberland; canal levelCCIV	432		
Bench Mark at Northumberland..	434		
Danville ; canal level	443		
Bloomsburg ; canal level........	470		
Below Berwick ; canal level	480		
Shickshinny ; canal level........	500		
Nanticoke dam	504		
Wilkesbarre ; canal level........	534		
Water in river above Wilkesbarre	511		
Top of coping Plainsville Lock...	541		

CCVI. Peach Bottom R. R.

Levels of the Peach Bottom R. R. were copied from notes in the office at York.

Datum : Susquehanna River at Peach Bottom, on the assumption that the water in the river at Peach Bottom stood at 85.88 feet above tide.

According to the profile of the Frederick Division of the Pa. R. R., the elevation of York above tide at Baltimore, is 364.6 feet. This is the latest determination. Sixteen feet have therefore been substracted to make the second column.

This R. R. is a 3 foot or "Narrow Guage," and connects with the Northern Central R. R. at York.

STATIONS.	Assumed Datum.	Corrected Tide.	
Susquehanna River Water	(85.88)	(70)	
Peach Bottom (*a*)	92.27	76	
Bangor Summit	511.23	495	
Delta	435.37	419	
Bryansville	241.36	225	
Woodbine	294.21	278	
Bridgeton	304.89	289	
Bruce	331.50	315	
Muddy Creek	366.86	351	
High Rock	382.93	367	
Laurel	411.62	395	
Fenmore	434.04	418	
Brogueville	478.19	462	
Felton	536.46	520	
Windsor	598.8	583	
Springvale	734.4	718	
Red Lion	912.31	896	
Dallastown	657.00	641	
Ore Valley	570.32	554	
Enterprise	531.20	515	
Smalls Mills	433.75	418	
Springgarden	431.53	415	
York ....CC,, IV CCVII	381.24	365	

a There is a Peach Bottom R. R. in Lancaster Co., branching from the Philadelphia and Baltimore Central, at Oxford, (see table CCLII,) and intended to connect with this line of York Co. at Peach Bottom, on the Susquehanna River.

CCVII. Pennsylvania Railroad, Frederick Division.

Levels of the Frederick Division, Pa. R. R., were copied from a profile of the road, in the office of the Pa. R. R. at Philadelphia, by permission of Mr. W. H. Brown, Engineer for Maintenance of Way.

Datum: Mean tide at Baltimore.

STATIONS.	Mean Tide.	Ocean Level.	
York (*a*) ....IV, CC	365		
Codorus Creek	357		
Graybills	426		
Bairs	452		
Spring Forge	455		
Menges Mill	455		
Iron Bridge	496		
Jacobs Mill	504		
R. R. Crossing (*b*)	607		
Hanover	599		
Conewago Bridge	546		
Littlestown	619		
Bridge	623		

a Junction with Northern Central; with York Branch of Columbia R. R.; and with Peach Bottom.

b Hanover Junction and Gettysburg R. R. Crosses at grade.

STATIONS.	Mean Tide.	Ocean Level.	
State Line	540		
Piney Creek	505		
Galts	486		
Taneytown	493		
R. R. Crossing (*c*)........CCLV	426		
Ladiesburg	464		
New Midway	458		
Woodsborough	400		
Georgetown	290		
Ritters	301		
Harmony Grove	310		
Frederick	280 (?)		
B. & O. Junction (*d*).....CCLVI	375		

c Western Maryland R. R., but *not at grade.*
d Connection with Baltimore and Ohio R. R.

CCVIII. Cumberland Valley R. R.

Levels on the Cumberland Valley R. R., were furnished by Mr. J. B. Dougherty, Engineer of the road at Chambersburg.

Datum: Originally a point on the Penna. R. R. at Harrisburg, foot of Market street, 315 feet above high water at Philadelphia.

STATIONS.	High Tide.	Ocean Level.	
Harrisburg (*a*)............I, CC	315	322	
Susq. Bridge, (west end) (*b*).....	350	357	
Shirmanstown			
Mechanicsburg	429	436	
Dillsburg Junction (*c*)......CCIX	420	427	
Kingston			
Middlesex			
South Mountain Junction (*d*)....	451	458	
Carlisle	470	477	
Greason's			
Newville	526	533	
Oakville			
Shippensburg	647	654	
Summit (*e*)	776	783	
Scotland			
Mount Alto Junction (*f*)........	707	714	
Chambersburg	611	618	
Marion			
South Pennsylvania Junction (*g*)	625	632	
Greencastle	578	585	
State Line			
Hagerstown	565	572	
Falling Waters			
Potomac Bridge	369	376	
Beddington			
Martinsburg (*h*) CCLVI	457	634	

a Junction with Penna. R. R., and with Northern Central R. R.
b Bridgeport. *c* Dillsburg Junction. *d* South Mountain R. R. Junction.
e Mount Alto R. R. Junction. *f* Southern Penna. R. R. Junction.
g Junction with Baltimore and Ohio R. R.

CCIX. Mechanicsburg and Dillsburg R. R.

Levels on the Mechanicsburg and Dillsburg R. R. were copied from notes in possession of Mr. J. B. Dougherty, Assistant Engineer on the Cumberland Valley R. R., at Chambersburg, Pa.

Datum: That of the Pa. R. R., high tide at Philada.

STATIONS.	High Tide.	Ocean Level.	
Mechanicsburg Junc. (*a*) CCVIII	420	427	
Dillsburg......................	536	542	

a With Cumberland Valley R. R. at Mechanicsburg, 8.5 miles west of Harrisburg.

CCIX bis. South Mountain R. R.

No levels of this road could be obtained. It runs south from Carlisle by Papertown, to Pinegrove Furnace, on Mountain Creek in the South Mountains.

STATIONS.			
Carlisle Junction (*a*) CCVIII			
Bonny Brook			
Craigh Head's.................			
Mount Holly Springs...........			
Upper (Paper) Mill............			
Hunter's Run..................			
Henry Clay			
Laurel			
Pinegrove (Furnace)...........			

CCX. Mount Alto R. R.

Levels on the Mount Alto R. R., were furnished by Mr. George B. Wiestling, Engineer and Superintendent.

Datum is "Elevation of Rail at foot of Market street, Harrisburg, 315.2 above high tide in Schuylkill River at Philadelphia."

This road runs to Mount Alto Furnace at the west foot of the South Mountain.

STATIONS.	High Tide.	Ocean Level.	
C. V. R. R. Junction (*a*).........	705	712	
Summit (*b*)	732	739	
Brookside (*c*)	700	707	
Woodstock (*d*).................	708	715	
Chambersburg Turnpike (*e*)	740	747	
Reno Ore Bank	875	882	
Mount Alto (*f*)	961	968	

a Junction with Cumberland Valley R. R., near Chambersburg.

b Between C. V. R. R. and Conochocheague Creek.

c At crossing of Creek.

d At crossing of Creek.

e Chambersburg and Gettysburg Turnpike,

f Near the Furnace.

CCX bis. Southern Pennsylvania R. R.

No levels could be obtained.

STATIONS.		Ocean Level.	
C. V. R. R. Junction (*a*) CCVIII			
Williamson....................			
Lehmaster's....................			
Mercersburg Junction............			
Loudon........................			
Richmond			
Mercersburg terminus			

a One mile south of Marion, and seven miles south of Chambersburg.

CCXI. Summit Branch R. R.

Levels of the Summit Branch R. R., were furnished by Mr. W. E. Ray, Supt. of the R. R., and cannot be relied upon as being entirely correct; but it is the only record which could be found of the road.

This road is called also the Lyken's Valley R. R.

Datum: Mean tide at Baltimore.

STATIONS.	Mean Tide.	Ocean Level.	
Millersburg (*a*).................	395		
Elizabethville..................			
Cross Road	660		
Lykenstown....................	675		
Wiconisco.................			
Big Lick Colliery			
Williamstown (*b*)	1125		

a On the Susquehanna River, east side; junction with Northern Central Railroad.

b Summit Branch Colliery. Connection broken for several miles with the Railroad from Brookside, past Good Spring, to Tremont and Pottsville.

CCXII. Selinsgrove and N. B. R. R.

Elevations on the line of the Selinsgrove and North Branch R. R. and of the Mifflintown Branch, of the same, were copied from notes in possession of Mr. W. A. Meeker, at Selinsgrove, Pa.

Datum assumed at a point on the D. L. & W. R. R. at Northumberland.

The second column gives the correlative heights above mean tide (Ocean level ?) at Baltimore.

NOTE. This R. R. has never been built. Only the preliminary line levels at the points named are given in the following table.

The line starts in Northumberland at the terminus of the Bloomsburg Division of the Delaware, Lackawanna & Western R. R., crosses the mouth of the West Branch Susquehanna, and keeps down the right bank of the Susquehanna River, to the mouth of the Juniata River (Table CCXII).

The other branch of the line strikes across country from Selinsgrove to the Juniata River at Mifflintown (Table CCXIII).

STATIONS.	Assumed Elevation.	Mean Tide.	Ocean Level.
Northumberland (*a*)..CLVCCXV	100	439	
River Road (*b*).................	86.4	426	
Keensville	84.9	424	
Selinsgrove (*c*)..................	88.7	428	
Burns dwelling house	67.9	407	
Pa. Canal (*d*)....................	70.6	410	
B. M., No. 16 (*e*)................	74.7	414	
Port Trevorton R. R. Tra k......	75.9	415	
Herrold's Saw Mill..............	63.3	403	
B. M., No. 18 (*f*)...............	72.6	402	
Wentzels Station................	66.3	406	
McKee's Half Falls..............	63.1	402	
Rines Store......................	60.2	400	
B. M., No. 21 (*g*)...............	60.6	400	
Mahontonga Creek (*h*)..........	38.2	378	
B. M., No. 23 (*i*)................	61.5	401	
B. M., No. 24 (*j*)	54.9	385	
B. M., No. 25 (*k*)..........	50.9	390	
Liverpool (*l*)	57.3	397	
Blattenberger's Mill	34.8	374	
Blattenberger's Creek (*m*)	16.4	356	
B. M., No. 27 (*n*)	31.4	371	
Montgomery's Creek (*o*)..........	14.5	354	
Girty's Notch Hotel	26.2	366	
B. M., No. 28 (*p*)...............	19.1	358	
New Buffalo (*q*)	24.6	364	
Buffalo Creek (*r*)	8.5	348	
B. M., No. 31 (*s*)	18	357	
Pittsburg Turnpike Crossing	15.2	355	
B. M., No. 33 (*t*)	—1.8	338	
Juniata River....................	-11.6	328	
Juniata Canal (*u*)................	18.4	358	
Pa. R. R. (*v*)	23.5	363	
B. M., No. 34 (*w*)...............I	19.6	359	

a Intersection with D. L. & W. R. R., at Northumberland.

b Opposite Northumberland.

c Centre of Pine Street.

d Top of mason work abutment of aqueduct, 2½ miles below Selinsgrove, crossing Penns Creek.

e Spike driven in telegraph pole, just above Port Trevorton.

f Below Port Trevorton, near two dwelling houses, on root of apple tree, 300′ from canal.

g 1500′ south of Benneville Kramer's house, on root of wild cherry tree.

h Surface of water, ordinary stage.

i 900′ north of Hoover's hotel, on chestnut tree.

j 2000′ south of "Dry Saw Mill" Hotel, piece of horse shoe, driven in telegraph pole.

k 500′ south of McCormick's barn, on root of elm tree.

l Centre of Market street.

m Surface of water.

n 900′ north of stone hotel, on root of black walnut tree.

CCXIII. *Mifflintown Branch S. & N. Br. R. R.*

NOTE. See last table CCXII.

STATIONS.	Assumed Elevation.	Mean Tide.	Ocean Level.
B. M., No. 1 (*a*)..........CCXII	101.2	441	
Kautz P. O. (*b*)	95.5	435	
Millers Mill.....................	134.4	474	
Freeburg.......................	157.2	497	
Apple's Brick House............	205.8	545	
Road (*c*).........................	263	602	
Cross Creek.....................	286.5	626	
B. M., No. 13 (*d*)................	375	714	
Shelly's Saw Mill (*e*)............	451.4	791	
Shelly's Summit................	453.2	793	
Richfield	412.6	752	
B. M., No. 14 (*f*)..............	408.7	748	
Cherryhill School House (*g*)	366.8	706	
Evansdale Summit..............	399	738	
Haldeman's Store (*h*)...........	377.4	717	
Bunkertown Church (*i*)	350.3	690	
Bunkertown	354.3	694	
Little Lost Creek (*j*)...........	355.4	695	
McAlistersville..................	308.6	648	
Leonard s Barn.................	262.9	602	
Wilson's Mill....................	227.2	566	
Wilson's Store...................	219.5	559	
Main Road (*k*)..................	224	563	
Banks Summit	270.6	610	
Happy Hollow School House (*l*)..	160.5	500	
Daniel Seiber's (*m*)..............	137.3	477	
Terminus of Line (*n*)..........I	109.2	449	

a Top of mile post No. 7, S. & L. R. R.
b Waters edge, ordinary low water, Middle Creek.
c Leading from Middleburg to Tremont.
d 1300′ west of Brick School House, root of white oak tree.
e Waters edge, head of Shelly's saw mill pond.
f Near rivulet.
g Public road crossing.
h Public road from Evansburg to Foutz Valley, opposite Haldeman's store.
i In public road, near Bunkertown Church.
j Surface of water.
k In main road, from McAlistersville to Mifflintown, one mile west of Oakland mills.
l Surface of water, creek or run, west of Happy Hollow school house.
m Surface of water in creek, at D. Seibers.
n Mifflintown, on large peg, with nail driven near corner of stable, at fence post.

---

o Surface of water.
p Point of rocks, foot of Girty's Mountain, spike driven in telegraph pole
q Water in mill race.
r Surface of water.
s 700′ south of J. Steel's dwelling house, on root of black walnut tree.
t 600′ south of Pittsburgh turnpike crossing, on root of hickory tree, on river bank.
u On towing path, Juniata Canal.
v On cross tie, Pa. R. R., near Duncannon.
w On top of locust stump, at edge of embankment of Pa. R. R.

CCXIV. *Shamokin Branch N. C. R. R.*

The elevations on Shamokin Branch of the Northern Central R. R., were furnished by Mr. A. B. Starr, Assistant Engineer P. & E. R. R.
Datum: Mean tide, Baltimore.

STATIONS.	Above Tide.	Ocean Level.	
Sunbury Junction (*a*)........CC	442		
Snydertown..................	497		
Shamokin....................	738		
Lancaster Branch (*b*)	831		
Mount Carmel................	1054		
End of Road.............. ...	1090		

a Junction with N. C. R. W., at Sunbury.
b Junction with Lancaster Branch.

CCXV. *Philadelphia and Erie R. R.*

The levels on the Philadelphia and Erie R. R. were copied from the notes in the office of the Company at Williamsport, Pa., by permission of Mr. A. B. Starr, Assistant Engineer. These levels were made subsequent to 1862. It is intended to re-level the road in 1876, for no reliance is placed on the levels in this Table by the Engineers of the road.
Datum: Mean Tide at Baltimore.

STATIONS.	Mean Tide.	Corrected Levels.	
Sunbury (*a*)..................CC	428.30		
D.H. & W.R.R. Junc. (*b*).CXVII	436.10		
Northumberland (*c*)........CLV	439.30		
Montandon (*d*)..............XIII	446.60		
Catawissa R.R. Crossing (*e*)..LXV	454.50		
Milton.......................	458.30		
Watsontown..................	465.62		
Dewart......................	470.40		
Catawissa R.R. Crossing (*f*) LXV	473.82		
Montgomery..................	474.10		
Muncy.......................	502.75		
Catawissa R.R. Crossing (*g*)..LXV	514.42		
Williamsport.................	510.43		
W. & E. (N. C.) Railroad Junction (*h*)............CCXVII	516.02		
Newberry....................	513.20		
Linden......................	517.21		

a Junction of Shamokin Branch of the Northern Central R. R.
b Junction Danville, Hazleton and Wilkesbarre R. R.
c Junction of Delaware, L. & W. R. R.
d Junction of Lewisburg, Centre & Spruce Creek R. R.
e Crossing of Catawissa R. R. near Milton.
f Crossing Catawissa R. R. near Montgomery.
g Crossing Catawissa R. R. below Williamsport.
h Junction with Northern Central R. W. near Williamsport.

STATIONS.	Mean Tide.	Corrected Levels.	
Susquehanna....................	516.60		
Jersey Shore....................	*577.07		
Pine....................	554.11		
Wayne....................	554.34		
Lock Haven (*i*).............XV	†538.91		
Queen's Run....................	565.05		
Farrandsville....................	564.63		
Ferney....................	576.44		
Glen Union....................	587		
Whetham....................	600.80		
Ritchie....................	614.34		
Hyner....................	626.30		
North Point....................	641.02		
Renova....................	653.90		
Westport....................	672.64		
Cook's Bun....................	691.43		
Keating....................	700.90		
Wistar................	720.72		
Round Island....................	736.81		
Grove....................	754.40		
Sinnemahoning....................	775.71		
Bennett's Br. Extension (*j*) CCCII	795		
Driftwood....................	797.75		
Huntley....................	842.93		
Sterling....................	896.38		
Cameron....................	943.73		
B. N. Y. & P. R.R. (*k*) CCXVIX	1003.09	(1024)	
Emporium....................	1014.99		
West Creek....................	1091.75		
Beechwood....................	1225.66		
Rathbon....................	1299.18		
Hemlock....................	1446.05		
West Creek Summit............	1677.64		
St. Mary's....................	1649.50		
Scahonda....................	1503.90		
Daguschahonda (*l*)............	1461.95		
Shawmut (*m*)....................	1408.56		
Ridgway....................	1375.73		
Johnsonburg....................	1423.52		
Wilmarth....................	1428.80		
Wilcox....................	1508.52		
Dahoga....................	1586.75		
Clarion Summit....................	2007.90		
Kane....................	2002.83		
Wetmore....................	1792.63		
Ludlow....................	1591.55		
Roy Stone....................	1403.75		

* Probably 557.07. † 558.91 ? See next Table below. See also the 555 of Table XV.

i Junction with Bald Eagle Valley R. R.

j Junction with the Bennett's Branch Extension of Allegheny Valley R. R.

k Junction with the Buffalo, New York & Philadelphia R. R.

l Here the Daguchahonda R. R. joins. No levels got.

m Shawmut R. R. No levels got.

STATIONS.	Mean Tide.	Corrected Levels.	
Sheffield	1325.70		
Tiona	1348.03		
Clarenden	1385.46		
Stoneham	1335.93		
Warren CCCVI	1182.60		
Oil Creek & A. V. R. R. Crossing CCCIV	1158.80		
Irvineton	1156.60		
Youngsville	1199.85		
Pittsfield	1233.31		
Garland	1297.47		
Spring Creek	1383.85		
Columbus	1389.18		
B.C.&P.R.R. Crossing (*l*) CCCIX	1429.20		
Corry	1419.58		
A.& G.W.R.R. Crossing (*m*) CCC	1415.92	(1439)‡	
Lovell's	1362.90		
Concord	1373.80		
Union	1258.63		
Lebeuff	1207.20		
Waterford	1181.72		
Jackson's	1218.70		
Langdon's	1123.52		
Belle Valley	995.96		
L. S. & M. S. Railroad Crossing (*n*) CCCLXXXIII	675.64		
Erie Depot CCCLXXXIV	(573)		
Lake Erie, Water	(565)	(573)‖	

l Crossing of the Buffalo, Corry and Pittsburgh R. R.

m Crossing of the Atlantic & Great Western R. R.

n Junction with the Lake Shore and Michigan Central at Erie.

‡ Level by the N. Y. & E. R. R.

‖ Accepted level of Lake Erie.

NOTE.—In the following Table some levels according to a profile made by John F. Burgin, Civil and Topographical Engineer, in 1862, are compared with levels of the same points found in Table CCXV above.

Column 1 shows Mr. Burgin's figures.

Column 2 shows the office figures.

STATIONS.	Above Tide.	Above Tide.	Difference.
Sunbury	423	428	+ 5
Milton	451	458	+ 7
Williamsport	506	510	+ 4
Lock Haven (*a*)	552	539	+ 7
De Crano	716		
2d Fork Sinnamahoning	787	798 ?	+11
Emporium	1011	1015	+ 4
Foot of Maximum Grade	1330		

a The 539 must be an error for 559.

STATIONS.	Above Tide.	Above Tide.	Difference.
West Creek Summit............	1682	1678	— 4
St. Mary's (*b*)..................	1628	1649	+21
Foot of Maximum Grade........	1518		
Ridgway (*c*)....................	1387	1376	— 9
Johnsonburg.....................	1429	1424	— 5
Wilcox..........................	1501	1509	+ 8
Foot of Maximum Grade........	1525		
Clarion Summit..........	2006		
Head of Two Mile Run..........	1914		
Foot of Maximum Grade........	1456		
Sheffield.........................	1324	1326	+ 2
Dutchman's Summit.............	1393		
Warren........	1189	1183	— 6
Irvine...........................	1162	1157	— 5
Youngsville....................	1203	1200	— 3
Pittsfield........................	1236	1233	— 3
Garland..........................	1298	1297	— 1
Spring Creek Station...........	1381	1384	+ 3
Columbus......................	1388	1389	+ 1
Corry............................	1416	1420	+ 4
Logan's Summit.......	1429		
Lovell's..........................	1363	1363	0
Concord.........................	1372	1374	+ 2
Union............................	1259	1259	0
Le Boeuf.........................	1205	1207	+ 2
Waterford.......................	1181	1182	+ 1
Jackson	1218	1219	+ 1
Langdon's.......................	1123	1124	+ 1
Belle Valley.....................	994	996	+ 2
Erie Depot.......................	573		
Lake Erie Surface (*d*)...........	565		

b Difference of 21 feet probably to be accounted for on the supposition that two different points are indicated, the gradients here being very steep.

c Head of the Clarion River, at the forks.

d The level of Lake Erie water was fixed by J. T. Gardner's Tables (U. S. Geol. and Geographical Survey of Colorado, for 1873, p. 635) "mean of observations from 1844 to 1857, 573.08;" adopted result at Cleveland, dependent upon repeated Erie Canal Levels and U. S. Coast Survey work.

CCXVI. Muncy Creek R. R.

The levels on the Muncy Creek R. R. were furnished by Mr. B. Morris Ellis, Treasurer.

Datum: Catawissa; (Reading) R. R. Mid tide at Philadelphia. Add 3 feet, for Ocean Level.

This R. R. line runs northeast, up Muncy creek to the top of the Allegheny or Great North Mountain table land of Sullivan County.

STATIONS.	Mean Tide.	Corrected Tide.	
Hall's Station (*a*) LXV	410	510	
*Hughesville (*b*)................	483	583	
Picture Rock......................	551	651	
Tivola............................	591	691	
Muncy Bottoms.....................	675	775	
Sonestown.........................	829	929	
McNeal's Summit (*c*).............	1676	1776	

a On Catawissa R. R. east bank of River.

b Mr. B. Morris Ellis, says, "This station is 80 feet higher than the Muncy Station (west side of river) on P. & E. R. R." called in Table CCXV, 502.75, and therefore, Hughesville is 582.75. Accordingly 100′ is added to Mr. Ellis' 483, and therefore to all other figures in the first column to make the second.

c This is the dividing ridge, between the Loyalsock and Muncy Creeks, which head within one-fourth mile of each other. It is known as McNeal's Summit, an engineer of that name having established a "bench" at this point many years since. It is two miles south of the town of Laporte (B. Morris Ellis).

Elevations of points in Sullivan County, Pa., furnished by Mr. B. Morris Ellis, of Hughesville, Pa.

In Cully township, in front of the hotel, at Long Pond, it is 2235′ above tide.

On the turnpike, one mile west of Long Pond, 2285′, the highest *known* point in Sullivan County.

At Lewis Lake, or Eagles Meare, it is 1726′.

CCXVII. Williamsport and Elmira R. R.

(NOW NORTHERN CENTRAL.)

Levels on this Northern Division of the Northern Central R. R. from Williamsport to Canandaigua, were copied from a profile in the office of the Company at Elmira. This road runs north up Lycoming creek.

Datum: Mean tide at Baltimore, Md.

STATIONS.	Mean Tide.	Ocean Level.	
Williamsport (*a*)..........CCXV	540		
Cogan Valley......................			
Crescent..........................			
Trout Run.........................			
Bodine's..........................			
Ralston...........................	860		
Roaring Branch....................			
Carpenter's.......................	1200		
Canton............................	1250		
Minnequa..........................	1230		
Alba..............................			
West Granville....................			
Granville Summit..................	1393		

a Junction with Philadelphia and Erie R. R.

STATIONS.	Mean Tide.	Ocean Level.	
Troy	1100		
Columbia Cross Roads			
Snedeker's			
Gillett's			
New York State Line			
Elmira (*b*) CLXII	865		
Horse Heads			
Pine Valley			
Mill Port			
Croton			
Havana	400		
Watkin's			
Rock Stream			
Starkey			
Himrod's			
Milo			
Pennyan			
Benton			
Hall's			
Stanley (*c*)			
Hopewell			
Canandaigua (*d*)	1070		

b Crosses New York and Erie R. R.
c Junction with Ontario and Southern R. R.
d Connects with New York Central and H. R. R. and Canandaigua and Tonawanda R. R.

CCXVIII. Jersey Shore, Pine Creek, and Buffalo R. R.

Levels on the J. S., P. Cr., and Buffalo R. R. were furnished by Mr. John S. Ross, Auditor. Datum: "Atlantic Ocean." This road is not yet built.

STATIONS.	Ocean Level.		
Williamsport, City limit (*a*) CCXV	502		
Linden (Surface of Canal)	501		
Larry's Creek (on Plank Road)	514		
Jersey Shore (Main Street)	521		
Pine Creek Crossing (Lentz)	532		
" " (Ramsey's Bend)	558		
Waterville (Surface Little Pine Cr)	587		
Jersey Mills	626		
Campbelltown	673		
Pine Cr. Crossing (near Slate Run)	709		
" " " Cedar "	760		
Babb's Creek Road	833		
Pine Cr. Crossing (ab. Marsh Cr.)	1106		
Gaines' (Water, Pine Creek)	1219		
Kilbourne's (Water, Pine Creek)	1274		
Grade at Summit of Tunnel	2202		
Coudersport	1634		
Roulette	1510		
Port Allegheny (*b*) CCXIX	1454		

a The Canal level at Williamsport, however is 509 according to Table CCIII.
b On Buffalo, N. Y. & Phila. R. R.—The difference between the Tables 1479—1454 = 25′ is unexplained.

CCXIX. *Buffalo, New York and Philadelphia R. R.*

Elevations on the B. N. Y. and P. R. R. were furnished by Mr. Geo. S. Gatchell, Engineer, who writes: "Calling Lake Erie 573′ above tide, *our* elevation at the crossing of the Erie Railway, at Olean, is 1435. Erie (R. R. levels) 1438, difference 3′. At Buffalo our elevation is 11′ above what we took to be surface of water in Lake Erie, but I do not think it is exactly right. We assumed surface of water in Lake Erie from surface of water in Buffalo Creek, about 3 miles from the Lake. Lake Erie, 573′; our depot, 11′ = 584; Erie Railway (levels) 588; difference 4′. You see the difference at Olean & Buffalo is very near the same. The Erie Railway here (at Olean), is on about the same elevation as our track."

STATIONS.	+Lake Erie	Above Tide	Erie R. R. Correction.
Emporium (*a*).....CCXV	448	1021	1024
Shippen..................	630	1203	1206
Keating (Summit)........	1305	1878	1881
Liberty.................	1070	1643	1646
Port Allegheny	906	1479	1482
Larabee's...............	905	1478	1481
Eldred..................	867	1440	1443
State Line..............	867	1440	1443
Portville...............	866	1439	1442
Olean (*b*).........CLXII	862	1435	1438
Hindsdale...............	880	1453	1456
Ischua..................	965	1538	1541
Franklinville...........	1017	1590	1593
Machias	1080	1653	1656
Yorkshire...............	882	1455	1458
Arcade..................	881	1454	1457
Protection..............	807	1380	1383
Holland.................	600	1173	1176
South Wales.............	414	987	991
Aurora..................	348	921	925
Jamieson................	317	890	894
Elma....................	250	823	827
Spring Brook............	180	753	757
Ebenezer................	63	636	640
Buffalo (*c*).............	11	584	588*

a On the Philadelphia and Erie R. R. where the unreliable list of the P. & E. R. R. makes the elevation 1003.09.

b Crosses New York & Erie R. R.

c Uses the same depot with the N. Y. & E. R. R., Lake Shore & M. S. R. R.

———. *Daguschahonda R. R.*

CCXX. *McKean and Buffalo R. R.*

Elevations on the McKean and Buffalo R. R. were furnished by Mr. S. V. Godden, Superintendent.

Datum: Lake Erie. To which must be added 573′ to reduce to Ocean Level.

The first column gives heights above an originally assumed Lake level. The second column corrects these heights for true Lake level.

STATIONS.	Above Lake Erie.	Above Lake Erie.	Above Tide.
Buff. N. Y. & P. R. R. (*a*) CCXIX	873.00	896.50	1469
Larabee's	871.50	895	1468
Frisbee	860.50	884	1457
Farmer's Valley	871.50	895	1468
Smethport	889.06	913	1486
Crosby	936.30	960	1533
Colegrove	938.80	962.30	1535
Hamlin	953.00	976.50	1549
Wernwag	1256.50	1280	1753
Clermont (*b*)	1469.50	1493	2066

a Junction with the Buffalo, New York and Philadelphia R. R. near Larabee's Station, on the Upper Alleghany River. *b* Bishop's Summit.

VI. SOUTHERN SERIES.

CCL. West Chester and Philadelphia R. R.

The levels of the West Chester and Philadelphia R. R., were copied from the profile, by permission of Mr. Thos. H. Hall, Treasurer of the Company.

Datum: Ordinary *low* water at Philadelphia. This is about the same as Ocean Level.

STATIONS.	Above Tide.	Ocean Level.
Philad'a Depot, 31st & Chestnut st	14	14
Woodland Street	57	57
Angora	74.5	74.5
Fernwood	90	90
Darby Road	103	103
Kelleyville	102	102
Clifton	109	109
Springhill	128	128
Morton	121.5	121.5
Swarthmore	125	125
Wallingford	168	168
Manchester	211.5	211.5
Media	210	210
Greenwood	218	218
Glen Riddle	160	160
Lenni	136	136
West Chester Junction (*a*) CCLII	133	133
Darlington	143	143
Glen Mill	199	199
Cheney	240	240
Street Road	252	252
Hemphill	318	318
West Chester	406	406

a With Philadelphia and Baltimore Central R. R.

CCLI. West Chester R. R.

Elevations of points on the West Chester Railroad, were copied from a profile made in 1831, in possession of Mr. Thos H. Hall, Treasurer, at the office of the Company, in Philadelphia. There is no location of the present stations on the profile, therefore the elevations in the following list, are given at the points where marked on the profile.

Datum: "Tide;" but a correction of 21 was needful; see note *b*; add 7 feet for Ocean level below P. R. R. datum.

STATIONS.	"Tide."	Corrected Tide.	Ocean Level.
West Chester			
Liberty Grove (*a*)	475.6	455	462
Goshen Street	474.6	454	461
Jones Hill	540	519	526
Ship Road	471	550	557
Steamboat Road	599.50	579	586
Summit	607.33	587	594
Malvern Junction P. R. R. (*b*)..I	560	539	546

a The starting point of the road in the *eastern* part of the town of West Chester.

b Junction with Pennsylvania R. R. at Malvern Station. The elevation of the Pa. R. R. at this point is + 539.258. The levels on West Chester Railroad have been reduced to correspond with Pa. R. R.

CCLII. Philadelphia and Baltimore Central R. R.

Levels on the Philadelphia and Baltimore Central Railroad, were copied from a profile furnished by Mr. H. Wood, Gen'l Supt.

Datum is said to be *mid tide* at Philadelphia = about Ocean level.

STATIONS.	Above Tide.	Ocean Level.	
Lamokin Junction CCLIII			
Rockdale			
Lenni			
West Chester Junction (*a*)..CCLI	133	133	
Chester Heights	234	234	
Patterson			
Woodland	212	212	
Concord	237	237	
Brandywine Summit	273	273	
Chadd's Ford	129	129	
Fairville	255	255	
Rosedale	312	312	
Kennett Square	260	260	
Toughkennamon	283	283	
Avondale	227	227	
West Grove	444	444	
Penn Station	506	506	
Elk View			
Lincoln University			
Oxford (*b*)			
Rising Sun			
Rowlandville			
Columbia & P. D. Junc.(*c*)CCLIV			

a With West Chester and Philada. R. R. *b* With Peach Bottom R. R.
c On the Susquehanna River above Port Deposit.

*** Peach Bottom R. R.*

STATIONS.			
Oxford Junction CCLII			
Hopewell			
Tweeddale			
Spruce Grove			
White Rock			
Kings Bridge			
Fairmount			
Fulton House..................			

** See CCVI.—Levels of this road wanting.

CCLIII. Philadelphia, Wilmington and Baltimore R. R.

Levels of the P. W. & B. R. R. were copied from the profile in the office of the Company at Philadelphia. Assumed level 94 feet too high.

Datum: Ordinary *low* water at Philadelphia = Ocean level.

STATIONS.	Profile.	Corrected Tide.	
Philadelphia....................			
Southwark	101.40	7.40	
Third Street	120.55	26.55	
Sixth Street................	126.78	32.78	
Seventh Street	127.58	33.58	
Tenth Street....................	126.26	32.26	
Twelfth Street.	120.59	26.59	
Eighteenth Street	129.66	35.66	
Newport Street..................	137.53	43.53	
Greys Ferry Bridge............	130.59	36.59	
Lazaretto	115.89	21.89	
Paschall			
Darby Street			
Sharon Hill			
Ridley Park.			
Chester Bridge (*a*)	118.33	24.33	
Lamokin Junc (*b*)........CCLII			
Thurlow	128.24	34.24	
Linwood........................	124.88	30.88	
Claymont	123.50	29.50	
Holly Oak	103.50	9.50	
Bellevue	108.07	14.07	
Wilmington LVI	101.11	7.11	
Delaware R. R. Junction			
Newport			
Staunton			

a Near Chester Station.

b Philadelphia and Baltimore Central R. R.

STATIONS.	Profile.	Assumed Elevation.	Corrected Tide.	
Newark	200.13	94	106.13	106
Iron Hill	216.70	94	122.70	123
Elkton	122.25	94	28.25	28
North East	137.75	94	43.75	44
Charlestown				
Perryville (c) CCLIV	115.48	94	21.48	21
Susquehanna (d)	110.34	94	16.34	16
Havre de Grace	110.12	94	16.12	16
Aberdeen	169.80	94	75.80	76
Perrymansville	136.39	94	42.39	42
Edgewood				
Magnolia				
Gunpowder Bridge	103.78	94	9.78	10
Chase's	114.40	94	20.40	20
Stemmer's Run				
Patapsco Neck	111.13	94	17.13	17
Bayview Junction (e)..CC	129.92	94	35.92	36
Baltimore Dep't (f) CCLVI	103.33	94	9.33	9

c Port Deposit Branch R. R.
d Susquehanna River, north-east side.
e Northern Central Railway Junction.
f Baltimore and Ohio R. R.

CCLIV. Columbia and Port Deposit R. R.

Elevations on the Columbia and Port Deposit R. R., were copied from a profile furnished by Mr. J. B. Hutchinson, Chief Engineer.
Datum: *Mean* tide at Port Deposit, nearly = Ocean level.

STATIONS.	A. M. T.	Ocean Level.	
Perryville (a) CCLIII		(21)	
Port Deposit	8	8	
P. & B. C. R. R. Junc. (b) CCLII	35	35	
Conomingo Creek	70	70	
Ball Friar	77	77	
Ark Haven	79	79	
Peach Bottom (c)	98	98	
Fishing Creek	108	108	
Fights Eddy	118	118	
McCalls Ferry	168	168	
York Furnace	176	176	
Shank's Ferry	182	182	
Safe Harbor	197	197	
Wislar's Run	228	228	
Washington	231	231	
Columbia (d)	240	240	

a Philadelphia, Wilmington and Baltimore R. R.
b Junction with Baltimore Central R. R.
c Peach Bottom R. R. starts from the opposite side of the Susquehanna River. See table CCVI.
d The elevation is in the lower part of Columbia, and is about 4′ lower than where the elevation is given on Pa. R. R. "Elevation on Pa. R. R. track in front of passenger station is 244′."

CCLV. Western Maryland R. R.

Elevations of the W. M. R. R., were copied from profile furnished through the kindness of Gen. J. M. Hood, President and Gen'l Manager of the road.
Datum: *Mean* tide at Baltimore = ? Ocean level.

STATIONS.	Tide.	Ocean Level.	
Baltimore, Canton Wharf........	20	20	
B. & P. R. R. Crossing (*a*)....CC	150	150	
Oakland			
Arlington			
Mount Hope....................			
Howardville			
Pikesville			
Greenwood			
McDonough.....................			
Junction.......................			
Owing's Mills..................	480	480	
Timber Grove..................			
Reisterstown...................	600	600	
Glen Morris....................			
Finksburg......................			
Patapsco.......................	360	360	
Shamberger's			
Parrs Ridge....................	680	680	
Tannery........................			
Westminster (*b*)...............	680	680	
Avondale			
Smith's Switch.................			
New Windsor	440	440	
Linwood			
Union Bridge...................	350	350	
Middleburg.....................			
Frederick Junction (*c*) ...CCVII			
Double Pipe Creek..............			
Monocacy River	280	280	
Rocky Ridge....................	370	370	
Loy's			
Graceham.......................			
Mechanicstown	475	475	
Sabillasville			
Blue Ridge Summit (*d*)	1373	1373	
Waynesborough			
Smithsburg.....................			
Chewsville.....................			
Antietam Creek.................	460	460	
Cumbl'nd Valley Junc.(*e*)CCVIII			
Hagerstown	520	520	
Williamsport...................	305	305	

a Baltimore and Potomac R. R. (or Northern Central) Crossing.
b Bachman's Valley R. R., no levels obtainable.
c Frederick Division of Penna. R. R. CCVII.
d Montery Springs Summit.
e Cumberland Valley R. R. Level in table CCVIII is feet.

CCLVI. Baltimore and Ohio R. R.

Levels on the B. & O. R. R., were copied from a profile and notes in the office of the Company at Baltimore, by permission of Mr. W. N. Bolling, Engineer.

Datum: The levels are based upon mid tide at Baltimore, and are according to the original survey of the road by Mr. B. H. Latrobe, Chief Engineer, many years ago.

It was impossible to get the levels at all the stations on the road.

STATIONS.	Mean Tide.	Ocean Level.	
Baltimore (Camden Station)......	24	24	
Mount Clair....................	66	66	
Winan's Station (*a*) CC			
Washington Junction (*b*)........			
Ellicotts Mills...	139	139	
Elysville........................			
Woodstock......................			
Marriottsville..................			
Sykesville......................			
Parr's Ridge....................	813	813	
Gaither			
Woodbine.......................			
Mount Airy			
Monrovia.......................			
Ijamsville			
Hartman's			
Frederick City Junc. (*c*) ...CCIX			
Monocay River..................	262	262	
Frederick City..................	280	280	
Doub's			
Point of Rocks (*d*)............	221	221	
Berlin			
Knoxville (*e*)			
Hagerstown Junction............			
Sandy Hook....................			
Harpers Ferry (*f*)............	272	272	
Duffield's			
Kearneysville..................			
Vanclieveville....			
Martinsburg....................			
Shepardstown Road	467	467	
North Mountain................	547	547	
Cherry Run....................	308	398	

a Baltimore and Potomac R. R. Crossing.

b Washington Branch B. & O. R. R. diverges from main line at this point.

c Frederick Branch B. & O. R. R.

d Metropolitan Branch B. & O. R. R. connects with main line. *No levels of this line.*

e Washington County Division B. & O. R. R. joins main line at this point. *No levels of this line.*

f Winchester, Potomac & Strassburg R. R. connects with B. & O. R. R. This is one of the R. R's of the State of Virginia.

STATIONS.	Mean Tide.	Ocean Level.
Sleepy Creek....................		
Hancock................(about)	424	424
Sir John's Run..................	434	434
Great Cacapon..................		
Willett's Run		
Rockwell's Run.................		
Doe Gully Tunnel	545	545
Little Cacapon..................	562	562
South Branch Potomac River....		
Green Spring Run		
Patterson's Creek...............	568	568
Cumberland (*g*)..........CCLIX	639	639
Brady's Mill....................		
Rawlings........................		
Black Oak Bottom		
New Creek		
Piedmont ....(about)	919	919
Bloomington....................	993	993
Frankville		
Swanton........................		
Altamont.......................	2620	2620
Deer Park......................		
Oakland		
Huttons........................		
Cranberry Summit..............	2550	2550
Rodermer's Tunnel..............		
Rowlesburg		
Cheat River....................	1397	1397
Cassady Summit................	1856	1856
Kingwood Tunnel	1820	1820
Tunnelton......................		
Newburg........................		
Independence		
Raccoon Run....................	1227	1227
Thornton.......................		
Grafton (*h*)	985	985
Fetterman		
Valley Falls....................		
Texas..........................		
Benton's Ferry.................		
Fairmount......................	888	888
Barnesville		
Barrackville...............		
Farmington.....................		
Mannington		
Glover's Gap...................	1150	1150
Glover's Gap Tunnel	1146	1146
Burton.........................		
Littleton..........		

g Pittsburgh and Connellsville Branch of B. & O. R. R. intersects main line here.

h Parkersburg Branch B. & O. R. R. diverges from main line at this point.

STATIONS.	Mean Tide.	Ocean Level.	
Board Tree Tunnel	1104	1104	
North Fork of Fish Creek	887	887	
Bellton.........................			
Welling Tunnel.................	1193	1193	
Cameron	1049	1049	
Easton's			
Roseby's Rock..................			
Moundsville (*i*)................	661	661	
McMechen's Cut................			
Benwood .... } South Bank of Wheeling Creek }	648	648	
Wheeling, High Water (*j*).......	637	(663)	

i Here the R. R. strikes the Ohio River bank and ascends hence to Bridgeport, opposite Wheeling; crosses by a bridge and continues west as Central Ohio Division of Baltimore and Ohio R. R.

j Wheeling.—Mr. J. T. Gardner, in his "Elevations of certain datum points," p. 655 of Hayden's Report of 1873, treats fully of the level of the Ohio River at Wheeling, in relation to the levels of the B. & O. R. R., and arrives at the "probable" conclusion that "the B. & O. R. R. results are too low," giving an improbable fall to the Ohio from Steubenville, exceeding 1 foot per mile, which is known to be its true rate of fall, from P. & S. R. R. and C. & P. R. R. surveys. High water at Wheeling is 637′ by B. & O. R. R. survey of 1832, and the "channel" is 588. This is about 30′ too low. Mr. Gardner makes Wheeling H. W. 1852.............................. about 663

CCLVII. Cumberland and Pennsylvania R. R.

Levels on the C. & P. R. R. were furnished by Mr. James A. Millholland, Vice-President of the Company, Cumberland, Md.

STATIONS.	Above Tide.		
Cumberland (*a*)..........CCLVI	650		
Eckert Branch Junction (*b*)......			
Mount Savage Junction (*c*)......			
C. & P. Junction (*d*)............			
Barrelville......................			
Mount Savage.................	1206		
Frostburg	1920		
Neff Run......................			
Lonacoming....................	1560		
Barton.........................			
Piedmont (*e*)..................	928		

a Baltimore and Ohio R. R.—Level of "Cumberland" in B. & O. R. R., Table CCLVI is 639, which, however, is Mr. Latrobe's original level.

b No levels.

c Bridgeport & Bedford R. R.

d Connellsville & Pittsburgh Branch B. & O. R. R.

e Rejoins the Baltimore & Ohio R. R.

NOTE.—This road runs back of the mountain, west of the river, through the Cumberland Coal Basin.

CCLVIII. Cumberland Turnpike Road.

Levels on the Cumberland Turnpike Road were copied from a report made by Jonathan Knight, Chief Engineer of the Baltimore and Ohio R. R., October 5th, 1835. They were partly taken from a map and profile made by James Schriver, in 1824. Mr. Knight says, in his report, "The levels may be sufficiently accurate for such a road (turnpike), yet are not so exact as levelings taken for a canal or railroad."

Datum: Probably mean tide at Baltimore.

NAMES OF TOWNS, &c.	Above Tide.	
Cumberland......CCLVI	635	
Frostburg	1890	
Great Savage Mountain Summit	2657	
Savage River, 2 miles from its head	2376	
Little Savage Mountain Summit	2535	
Little Backbone Mountain Summit at (Beall's) Dividing Eastern and Western Waters	2372	
Meadow Mountain Summit (Alleghany Mtn.)	2654	
Castelman's River	2077	
Negro Mountain Summit	2826	
Keyser's Ridge Summit, a spur of Negro Mountain	2843	
Winding Ridge Summit	2534	
Smythfield at Youghiogheny River	1405	
Barren Hill Summit	2450	
Woodcock Hill or Briery Mountain	2500	
Laurel Hill or Most Western Mountain	2412	
Munroe at Western Base of Laurel Hill	1065	
Uniontown	952	
Cauley's Hill	1274	
Brownsville at Monongahela River	873	
Hillsborough	1750	
Washington	1406	
West Alexandria	1797	
Wheeling	748	

CCLIX. Pittsburgh and Connellsville R. R.

Levels on the P. & C. Branch of the B. & O. R. R. were copied from the profile in the office of the Company at Connelsville, Fayette County, Pa.

Datum: As noted on the profile is 200′ *below low water at Pittsburgh*, and 514′ *above mean tide;* therefore 514′ has been added to each elevation, as copied from the profile to get mean tide at Baltimore = ? ocean level.

STATIONS.	Assumed Elevation.	Mean Tide.	
Cumberland (*a*)..........CCLVI	124	638	
Mt. Savage Jun. (*b*)(*c*)IX.CCLVII.	170	684	

a With B. & O. R. R.
b Cumb. & Pa. R. R.
c Bedford & Bridgeport R. R.

STATIONS.	Assumed Elevation.	Mean Tide.	
Ellerslie	216	730	
Cook's Mills	270	784	
Bridgeport	424	938	
Fairhope	870.5	1385	
Southampton	104.5	1564	
Glencoe	1119	1633	
Philson's	1347	1861	
Sandpatch Tunnel	1712	2226	
Summit	1772	2286	
Myersdale (*d*) CCLX	1549	2063	
Garrett (*e*) CCLXI	1433.5	1948	
Pinegrove	1360	1874	
Mineral Point (*f*) CCXII	1310.9	1825	
Castleman	1142.6	1757	
Pinkerton	1135	1649	
Shoo-Fly Tunnel	1100	1614	
Brook Tunnel	1044	1558	
Ursina (*g*)			
Confluence	832	1346	
Draketown Run	805	1319	
Egypt	788	1302	
Ohio Pyle	723	1237	
Indian Creek	468	982	
Sand Works	407	921	
White Rock (*h*) CCLXIII	407	921	
Connellsville (*i*) CCLXVI	380	849 –	
Broad Ford (*j*) CCLYIV	358	872	
Sedgwick	354	868	
Dawson (*k*) CCLXV	350	864	
Laurel Run	342	856	
Oakdale	338	852	
Layton	304	818	
Barring's	290	804	
Jacob's Creek	280	794	
Smith's Mill			
Port Royal	278	792	
Snyder's	274	788	
West Newton	268	782	
Sewickley (*l*) XXXI		(780)	
Armstrong's	265	779	
Robbin's	254	768	
Coultersville	254	768	
Alpsville	254	768	
Osceola	254	768	

d Salisbury & Baltimore R. R. Junction.
e Buffalo Valley R. R.
f Somerset & Mineral Point R. R.
g Coal R. R.
h Fayette and Uniontown Branch R. R.
i S. W. Pa. R. R.
j Mt. Pleasant Branch.
k Hickman Run Branch R. R.
l Youghiogheny R. R., Branch of Pa. R. R. difference of 1' in levels at Sewickley.

STATIONS.	Assumed Elevation.	Mean Tide.	
Ellrod	254	768	
Long Run	251	765	
McKeesport	251	765	
Riverton	251	765	
Saltsburg	251	765	
Port Perry Junction	251	765	
Braddock's	255	769	
City Farm	247	761	
Salt Works	252	766	
Brown's	243	757	
Grove	270	784	
Hazelwood	275	789	
Frankstown	269	783	
Laughlin	256	770	
Copper Works	249	763	
Soho	255	769	
Birmingham Bridge	237	751	
Pittsburgh	237	751	

CCLX. Salisbury R. R.

Levels on the Salisbury R. R. were furnished by Mr. R. I. Batzer, C. E.
Datum: Pittsburgh and Connellsville R. R. at Meyersdale.
This road runs south up Castleman's River, towards the Maryland line.

STATIONS.	Mean Tide.		
Pitts. & Conn. R. R. Junction (*a*) CCLIX	2095		
Meyersdale	2063		
Coal Mines (*b*)	2067		
Romain	2073		
Keystone	2075		
Livengood's Mill	2100		
Salisbury	2131		
Coal Mines (*c*)	2331		

a Junction with Pittsburgh and Connellsville R. R. near Meyersdale, or Myer's Mills.
b Cumberland and Elklich Coal Mines.
c Salisbury and Baltimore Coal Mines.

CCLXI. Buffalo Valley R. R.

Elevations on the Buffalo Valley R. R. were furnished by Mr. S. Philson, President of the Company.
Datum: Pittsburgh and Connellsville R. R.
This road runs north into Somerset County.

STATIONS.	Mean Tide.		
Garrett (*a*)..............CCLIX	1947		
Burkholder....................	1992		
Beaghley's....................	2010		
Bitner........................	2044		
Pine Hill.....................	2064		
Hanger's......................	2073		
Berlin........................	2176		

CCLXII. Somerset R. R.

NOTE.—The records of this road were destroyed by fire. It runs north into Somerset County towards Johnstown.

CCLXIII. Fayette Branch, P. & C. R. R.

Levels on this Branch of the Pittsburgh and Connellsville R. R. were copied from a profile in the office of the Company at Connellsville, Pa., through the kindness of Mr. W. H. Taylor, Resident Engineer.

Datum: Mean tide at Baltimore, Md.

This road runs southwest along the west foot of Chestnut Ridge towards the Virginia State line.

STATIONS.	Mean Tide.		
White Rock (*a*)..........CCLIX	907		
Fayette.......................	924		
Watt's........................	991		
Dunbar........................	1011		
Ferguson......................	1138		
Mt. Braddock..................	1175		
Lemont's......................	1084		
Evans'........................	1009		
Hoggsett's....................	978		
Uniontown.....................	981		

a Junction with Pittsburgh & Connellsville R. R. just above Connellsville.

NOTE.—The other bridge (at Connellsville) carries the southwest Pennsylvania R. R., which also runs up Dunbar Creek to Uniontown.

CCLXIV. Mt. Pleasant Branch, P. & C. R. R.

Data obtained as the last mentioned.

This road runs northeast along the west foot of Chestnut Ridge.

STATIONS.	Mean Tide.		
Broad Ford (*a*)..........CCLIX	873		
Morgan's........................	944		
Tinstman's	1076		
Valley Coal Mines	1035		
Fountain Mills..................	1040		
West Overton....................	1045		
Iron Bridge.....................	1052		
Stauffer's......................	1057		
Mt. Pleasant....................	1086		
End of Road.....................	1083		

a Junction with Pittsburgh and Connellsville R. R. at Broad Ford, 3.2 miles below Connellsville.

CCLXV. Hickman's Run Branch, P. & C. R. R.

Data as above.

This road, one mile long, runs north to Coke Banks.

STATIONS.	Above Tide.		
Dawson Junction (*a*).....CCLIX	872		
Terminus of Road...............	1006		

a Junction with Pittsburgh and Connellsville R. R. near Dawson.

CCLXVI. Southwest Pennsylvania Extension.

Levels on the Extension of Southwest Penna. R. R. were furnished by Mr. John C. Oliphant, Engineer.

Datum is *high tide* in Schuylkill River, at Philadelphia. Add 7′ for ocean level. For the surveys an artificial datum was assumed, as shown in column 1. Column 2 gives this corrected for high tide at Philadelphia. Column 3 corrected for ocean level.

The main road is given in the I series, Table XXX.

This road crosses the Youghiogheny at Connellsville, and keeps up Dunbar Creek over to Uniontown, parallel with the Fayette County Branch of the P. & C. R. R. See Table CCLXIII.

STATIONS.	Assumed Elevation.	Above Tide.	Ocean Level.
Connellsville (*a*).........CCLIX	159.5	908	915
Sub-grade, Pier No. 1...........	153.6	902	909
Ordinary Water in Youghiogheny River, at R. R. Bridge, S. W. Penna. R. R................	118	866	873

a Crosses *above* P. & C. R. R. here on a Bridge.

STATIONS.	Assumed Elevation.	Above Tide.	Ocean Level.
New Haven	138	886	893
Wheelerville	144	892	899
Dunbar	246.4	995	1002
Ferguson	376.2	1125	1132
Mt. Braddock (*b*)	448	1196	1203
Lemont	274.8	1023	1030
Hoggsett's Mill	205.7	954	961
Uniontown (*c*)	234.2	983	990

b Deep Cut; original surface 485 + 748.5 = 1233.5
c Intersection of Main Street and Broadway.

CCLXVII. Youghiogheny Coal Mine Levels.

Elevations of *Coal openings* on the line of Youghiogheny R. R. furnished by Mr. I. F. Wolf, Engineer Penn Gas Coal Company.

Datum: That of the Pa. R. R.

Youghiogheny Mine, No. 1	720.40
" " " 2	776.40
" " " 4	800.40
Th. Moore's drift at Moore's station P. & C. R. R.	793.40
Markel's Drift at Junction of Yough. R. R	824.44

CCLXVIII. Westmoreland Levels.

Various datum points in Westmoreland County, Pennsylvania, from a survey made by Mr. F. Z. Shellenberg, Superintendent of the Westmoreland Coal Company, Irwin's Station, Penna. R. R.

Datum: That of the Pennsylvania R. R. (Add 7′ for Ocean Level.)

Long Run Presbyterian Church Bench Mark on Door Sill	+ 1150′
Circleville Intersection of Mount Pleasant Turnpike with Greensburg and Pittsburgh Turnpike	1223
Jacksonville. Turnpike east end of town	1152
South Side Mine Mouth Coal	898
Larimer's Coal Mine	961
Ray's Coal Bank; on farm of William Ray's heirs	1052
Robinson's Coal Bank; on farm of R. S. Robinson	989
Bigley's Mines; Mouth of Drain, entry from Armstrong's Osceola Works, P. & C. R. R., at head of Bigley's Main Entry	902
Coal Hollow: Youghiogheny Coal Hollow Coal Company's Mines, between Guffey's and Shaner's Station, P. & C. R. R. Coal	789
Armstrong's Coal, opposite Buena Vista (east)	813
Moore's Coal Mine	812
Suter's Station, P. & C. R. R. Coal	843
Westmoreland Coal Shaft (Coal?)	751
Foster Shaft (Penn Township). Coal	935
Penn Coal Mine, north side of Penn Station, Pa. R. R	927
Kifer's Coal Bank, east of Penn Station, north side of Pa. R. R.	1140
Smith's Coal Bank	1180
Loughner's Coal Bank	1102

Harrison City, two miles north of Manor Station, on Pa. R. R., on *bridge* over Brushy Run 967
Cross Roads, two miles west of Harrison City 1185
Salem : *Intersection* of Freeport and Saltzburg Roads, northeast of Salem. 1231
Salem : Burnt Cabin *Summit*, between Allegheny and Monongahela Waters, between Beaver Run and Turtle Creek, one-half mile northeast of Salem. 1200
Salem Cross Roads (Delmont P. O.). 1255
Salem : Coal at Salem Cross Roads. 1272
Bouquet Village *Road*, opposite Grist Mill 1102
Bouquet Coal 1104
William Duff's Steam Grist Mill, *surface of water* just below Mill. . . 950
King's Bank, Coal at Burnt Cabin Summit. 1203
McQuade's Coal Bank on road leading from Salem Cross Roads to Freeport 1189
John Cochran's Coal Bank. 1132
Thorn Run : *Water* in Run at road crossing Jas. Cochran's farm. . . . 1080
Turtle Creek : *Water* in Creek at northern turnpike crossing, on Waugaman's farm 1051
Turtle Creek : Northern *turnpike* crossing, at Long's. 995
Turtle Creek : *Water* in Creek at Remaly's Mill. 950
Walton's *Summit*, between waters of Turtle Creek and Brushy Run . 1194
Longacre's *Summit* 1187
Brinker's *Summit* 1202
Fink's Run : *Water* at junction with Brushy Run, four miles north of Manor Station, Pa. R. R 1000

CCLXIX. Pittsburgh, Virginia and Charleston R. R.

Levels on the P. V. & C. R. R. were copied from the profile in the office of the company at Pittsburgh, by permission of I. M. Byers, Esq., Superintendent.

Datum :

This road ascends the west bank of the Monongahela River from Pittsburgh to the Virginia State Line, and is in process of completion above Monongahela City. It crosses the river from Pittsburgh to Birmingham on a high bridge.

STATIONS.	Above Tide.	Ocean Level.	
Pittsburgh (*a*)..........CCCLII	750		
12th Street, Birmingham.........	786		
18th " "	779		
22nd " "	770		
30th " "	745		
Beck's Run....................	750		
Bird's Run....................	749		
Street's Run..................	745		
West's Run....................	740		
Homestead.....................	745		
Patterson's Run...............	742		
Opposite Braddock's...........	730		
Thompson's....................	749		
Opposite McKeesport...........	725		
Curry's Run (*b*)	734		

a Junction with the Pittsburgh, Cincinnati and St. Louis R. R.
b On bridge.

STATIONS.	Above Tide.	Ocean Level.	
Camden	738		
Rock Run	731		
Pine Run	739		
Peter's Creek	735		
Wylie's	743		
Elizabeth	731		
Walton's	741		
Hodgen's Coal Road	735		
Coal Bluff Road	735		
Houston's Run	740		
Buffalo Coal Works	748		
Mingo Creek	740		
Dry Run	735		
Monongahela City	737		
Pigeon Creek (*c*)	735		
Johnson's Coal Road	750		
Pike Run	719		
West Brownsville (*d*)	758		

c Surface of water at ordinary stage 709.
d In Street in front of Hotel.

VII. ALLEGHENY SERIES.

CCC. Pittsburgh City Levels.

Elevations at different points in the City of Pittsburgh, Pa., were furnished by Mr. William Martin, Assistant Engineer.

Datum: *Low water in the Allegheny River* at the Suspension Bridge, which according to Mr. Jas. T. Gardner's determination, is 699.20′ above the Mean Surface of the Atlantic Ocean. See page 655, Vol. I, Hayden's Geological Survey Report of 1873.

Elevation of Points in City of Pittsburgh, Pa.

BENCH MARKS.	City Datum.	Ocean Level.	
On Window-sill of Monongahela Incline Plane, Check House	407.075	1106.275	
On Belt-course of Union Depot, Main Entrance	47.203	746.403	
On East end Door-sill of Point Breeze Hotel at Intersection of Penn and Fifth Avenue	273.814	973.014	
On Belt-course of Munshall's Distillery, corner Penn Avenue and Water Street	28.198	727.398	
On Door-sill of Post Office	51.554	750.754	
On Embankment of *Lower* (old) Reservoir on Bedford Avenue	165.854	865.044	
On Embankment of *Upper* (old) Reservoir, Bedford Avenue	401.674	1100.874	

BENCH MARKS.	City Datum.	Ocean Level.	
On Flow Line of Highland Avenue (new) Reservoir........	365	1064.20	
On Flow Line of Herron Hill (new) Reservoir..................	560	1259.20	
On Flow Line of Brilliant Hill (new) Reservoir............	235	934.20	

CCCI. Allegheny Valley R. R.

Levels on the Allegheny Valley R. R., from Kittaning to Oil City, were copied from notes in possession of Mr. Wainwright, Assistant Engineer, Engineer's Office, Allegheny Valley R. R., Pittsburgh, Pa.

This portion of the road was leveled during the summer of 1875. The elevation at Kittaning was assumed to be 500′ above tide. The difference between the true elevation and the elevation assumed at the Red Bank intersection of the Bennett's Branch R. R. with the main line, was made to be 284′. This must be incorrect.

Great difficulty has been experienced in connecting the levels of this road with those of others in Northwestern Pennsylvania, and no reliance can be placed upon their exactness. They are evidently *too low*, and the error seems to be in the 284′ feet difference; and therefore in the Bennett's Branch Extension Table, CCCII.

For instance, the level at Parker's City is, by this Allegheny Valley R. R. Table, 579.2 + 284 = 863′; whereas, Mr. Lucas makes it 909′, or 46 feet higher. See Section in Carll's Report of Progress, 1874.

Again, at Franklin this Table gives 678.5 + 284 = 963′; whereas, Lake Shore and Michigan Southern (Franklin Division) Table CCCLXII makes it 444.06 (+ Lake Erie) + 573 = 1017′, or 54 feet higher.

Again, at Oil City this Table gives 983′; whereas Oil Creek and Allegheny Valley R. R. (CCCIV) gives 995′, or 12′ higher. And the same in CCCLXXXVII by the Franklin Branch of Atlantic and Great Western.

The levels of points from Pittsburgh up to Kittaning could not be obtained by any efforts. There seem to be no records, profiles or notes of the levels of this part of the line. Pittsburgh is 745′ by Table I; Gardner makes it 746′, and so does Pittsburgh, Fort Wayne and Chicago R. R., Table CCLXXIII.

STATIONS.	Assumed	Tide.	Ocean Level.	
Pittsburgh.............			(745)	
Sharpsburgh............				
Hulton..................				
Logan's Ferry..........				
Parnassus...............				
Tarentum...............				
Chartiers...............				
Soda Works............				
West Penn Junction (*a*) XXVI..............			(778)	
White Rock............				

a With West Penn. R. R. east to Philadelphia.

STATIONS.	Assumed	Tide.	Ocean Level.	
Kelly's................				
Logansport............				
Rosston................				
Kittaning..............	500	784	791	
Cowanshannock.........	498.8	783	790	
Pine Creek.............	502.2	786	793	
Templeton	513.9	798	805	
Mahoning..............	514.4	799	806	
Reimerton..............	526.8	812	819	
Red Bank Junc. (*b*) CCCII	540.9	825	832	
Phillipsburg............	545.3	829	836	
Brady's Bend..........	546.4	831	838	
Catfish.................	548.5	833	840	
Sarah Furnace..........	551.5	836	843	
Hillsville..............	555.3	839	846	
Monterey...............	564.7	849	856	
Parker City (*c*)...CCCIII	579.2	863	870	
Foxburg	586	870	877	
Emlinton..............	595.2	879	886	
Dotterer's.............	604.9	889	896	
Black's................	612.6	897	904	
Rockland...............	616.6	901	908	
St. George's............	624.9	909	916	
Scrub Grass............	637.7	922	929	
Brandon's.	651.4	936	943	
Foster.................	659.8	944	951	
East Sandy............	665.4	950	957	
Cochran...............	672.5	957	964	
Franklin(*d*) } CCCLXV CCCLXII	678.5	963	970	
† Oil City (*e*)....CCCIV	699.2	983	990	

b Junction of Bennett's Branch R. R. Elevation according to profile of Bennett's Branch Ext. of Allegheny Valley R. R. + 821.70, which gives the above mentioned difference of 284′, used for reducing the other levels to tide This however depends on the Phila. & Erie R. R. levels, Table , which are as unreliable as those of the Allegheny Valley R. R. The connection between Harrisburg and Pittsburgh, round by the West Branch Susquehanna River, is divisible into three sections, the middle one (Bennett's Branch Extension R.R.) alone being reliable.

c Junction with Parker and Karn's City R. R.

d Junction with Atlantic and Great Western R. R., and with Lake Shore and Michigan Southern (Franklin Division) R. R.

e South Oil City, river rail, main track, opposite lower end of platform of depot. Junction with Oil City and Allegheny Valley R. R.

NOTE.--Seven feet has been added to the second column in the above Table to make the third column agree with levels in Table CCCII.

CCCII. Bennett's Branch Extension R. R.

The levels on the Bennett's Branch Extension, A. V. R. R., were copied from the profile in the office of the A. V. R. R. at Pittsburgh, Pa., through kindness of Mr. H. Blackstone, Chief Engineer.

Datum: Tide water at Philadelphia.

This datum, however, is dependent upon the level of the eastern terminus or Driftwood Junction with the Phil. & Erie R. R. But this is known to be too low, and therefore, the levels of the whole line are too low, and carry down with them those of the Allegheny Valley Main Line, as stated in notes, to Table CCCI.

Mr. Burgin's original level on the P. & E. R. R. at Driftwood was 788'. This Mr. Wilson took for his datum level in the surveys of the Bennett's Branch Extension R. R. across to the Allegheny Valley R. R. Mr. Wilson's levels are given in column 1.

On the profile of the P. & E. R. R. used in Table CCXVI, the level of the point of junction is called 795 (7 feet higher). Column 2 makes this first correction, which helps to lift the Allegheny Valley levels a little, but not near enough.

Column 3 is left blank for a future correction, when the levels of the P. & E. R. R. are lifted, as they must be; for, although they start about right at Sunbury, they are already about 20 feet too low at Williamsport by the Catawissa R. R. (LXV), and by the Northern Central R. R. (CC) lists of levels; and feet too low at Lock Haven by the Pennsylvania R. R. (XV) branch lists. At Emporium also they are 18 feet lower than the Buffalo, N. Y. & Phil. Railroad (CCXIX).

But even this 20 feet added to the previous 7' = 27' will not suffice to lift the west end of this Bennett's Br. Ext. R. R. high enough to cancel the difference at Franklin and Oil City. It is probable, however, that the whole residual error lies on the Allegheny Valley R. R. line.

STATIONS.	Above Tide.	Above Tide.	Corrected Tide.	Ocean Level.
Driftwood Junction (*a*) CCXVI	788	795		
Mix Run	848	855		
Miller's	880	887		
Dent's Run	898	905		
Enz	938	945		
Grant	949	956		
Mount Pleasant	973	980		
Devil's Elbow	993	1000		
Benezette	1014	1021		
Meadic's Run (*b*)	1073	1080		
Caledonia Tunnel (*c*)	1122	1129		
Slabtown Dam	1163	1170		
Hebner's Run	1245	1252		
Clear Run	1385	1392		
Slab Run	1381	1388		
Fall's Creek	1381	1388		
Crooked Run	1378	1385		
Evergreen	1374	1381		
Maghee's	1361	1368		
Panther's Run (*d*)	1362	1369		
Reynoldsville	1351	1358		
Prior Run (*e*)	1342	1349		
Prindible's	1335	1342		

a With P. & E. R. R. near Driftwood. "795" on P. & E. profile.
b Bench mark on Bridge; West abutment, top of Cap-stone, N. E. corner.
c 250' east of Tunnel.
d Cap-stone of east Abutment.
e Cap-stone of east Abutment.

STATIONS.	Above Tide.	Above Tide.	Corrected Tide.	Ocean Level.
McAnnutty Run (*f*)....	1335	1342		
Camp Run..............	1317	1324		
Fuller's Mill............	1301	1308		
Wolf Run..............	1295	1302		
Cable Run..............	1285	1292		
Iowa Mill..............	1273	1280		
Gooseneck..............	1256	1263		
Bell's Mill..............	1340	1347		
Garrison's Mill..........	1235	1242		
Brookville..............	1209	1216		
Nicholson's Mill........	1199	1206		
Corder's Run............	1200	1207		
Puckerty Point..........	1189	1196		
Rattlesnake Run........	1183	1190		
Baxter's Mill............	1181	1188		
Heathville..............	1137	1144		
Motter's Run............	1124	1231		
Bear Tree Run..........	1107	1114		
Maysville..............	1082	1089		
Pine Run..............	1075	1082		
Millville................	1067	1074		
Indiantown Run........	1063	1070		
Middle Run............	1060	1067		
New Bethlehem..........	1054	1061		
Anthony's Neck........	1025	1032		
Leatherwood............	1001	1008		
Rock Run..............	940	947		
Buck Lick Run..........	913	920		
Lawsonham (*g*)..........	893	900		
Fiddler's Run..........	889	896		
Red Bank Jun. (*h*) CCCI	825	832		

Sligo Branch of A. V. R. R.

STATIONS.	Above Tide.	Above Tide.	Corrected Tide.	Ocean Level.
Lawsonham (*i*)...CCCII	891	898		
Stop's Run............	913	920		
Fiddler's Run (*j*).......	966	973		
9000 feet (*k*)............	1043	1050		
14,000 feet..............	1141	1148		
15,000 feet..............	1161	1168		
17,000 feet..............	1202	1209		
23,000 feet..............	1325	1332		
Benn's Summit..........	1368	1375		
29,000 feet..............	1305	1312		
Cherry Run............	1198	1205		

f Cap-stone of west Abutment.
g Sligo Branch R. R.
h With Allegheny Valley R. R.
i Junction.
j First crossing; centre of Trestle.
k From the Junction.

STATIONS.	Above Tide.	Above Tide.	Corrected Tide.	Ocean Level.
38,000 feet............	1218	1225		
Sligo Summit...........	1300	1307		
Iron Ore Bank..........	1228	1235		
52,000 feet............	1150	1157		
Little Licking Creek....	1122	1129		
Big Licking Breek......	1102	1109		
Sligo (*l*)............	1090	1097		
End of Road...........	1085	1092		

Boston Branch of A. V. R. R.

STATIONS.	Above Tide.	Above Tide.	Corrected Tide.	Ocean Level.
Junction (*m*).....CCCII	1049	1056		
Bridge................	1050	1057		
2,000 feet.............	1075	1082		
3,000 feet.............	1097	1104		
4,000 feet.............	1118	1125		
5,000 feet.............	1138	1145		
6,000 feet.............	1161	1168		

l Sligo Furnace is served by this road.

m There are no stations marked on the profile of this branch. The levels are given at thousand feet from the point of divergence from the main road.

CCCIII. Parker and Karns City R. R.

Levels of the Parker and Karns City R. R. were taken from notes in possession of Mr. Wm. M. Kipp, Engineer at Parker City. The datum of the preliminary survey was an assumed level 100 feet below the top of the west abutment of the iron bridge then building. This datum (as shown by subsequent surveys in locating the line) is 103.99′ below the top of the free-stone base of the toll house. The bridge rises 8′ going east, and there is a further rise from the end of the bridge to the A. V. R. R. depot of 1.98′, as ascertained by Mr. J. F. Carll, which will make the datum of P. & K. C. R. R. below the A. V. R. R. depot 103.99 + 8 + 1.98 = 113.97′. Elevation A. V. R. R. depot, Parker City 863 — 114 = 749 = datum which added to the elevations as copied from notes should bring levels to tide.

STATIONS.	Above Tide.	Above Tide.	Ocean Level.	
Parker Junc. (*a*)..CCCI		863	870	
Stone House...........	315	1064	1071	
Martinsburg...........	330	1079	1086	
Argyle................	386.80	1136	1143	
Petrolia..............	401	1150	1157	
Central Point..........	410	1159	1166	
Karns City............	430.33	1179	1186	

a With Allegheny Valley R. R.

NOTE.—Seven feet has been added to the second column in the above Table to make the third column agree with Tables CCCI and CCCII.

CCCIV. *Oil Creek and Allegheny River R. R.*

Levels on the Oil Creek and Allegheny River R. R. were copied from the profile in the office of the Company, at Oil City, by permission of C. J. Hepburn, Esq., Superintendent.

Datum: P. & E. R. R.

STATIONS.	Above Tide.	Ocean Level.	
Irvincton (*a*)............CCXV	1158		
Dunn's Eddy..................	1144		
Penna. House..................	1140		
Thompson's..................	1130		
Cobham..................	1121		
Magee..................	1118		
Tidioute..................	1099		
Trunkeyville..................	1085		
Hickory..................	1078		
Dawson..................	1063		
Jamison..................	1060		
Tionesta..................	1047		
Hunter..................	1048		
Stewart..................	1034		
President..................	1035		
Eagle Rock..................	1033		
Henry's Bend..................	1022		
Oleopolis..................	1019		
Walnut Bend..................	1010		
Rockwood..................	1003		
Imperial..................	995		
Oil City............CCCLXVII	995		
McClintock..................	1045		
Rouseville..................	1026		
Rynd Farm..................	1030		
Tarr Farm..................	1049		
Columbia..................	1054		
Petroleum Centre..................	1076		
Boyd Farm..................	1073		
Pioneer..................	1086		
Shaffer..................	1120		
Miller's Farm..................	1118		
Titusville............CCCVIII	1181		
Hydetown..................	1239		
Bridge (*b*)..................	1241		
Gray's Mills (*c*)..........CCCVII	1266		
Meyer's Switch..................	1230		
Tryonville..................	1305		
Centreville..................	1284		
Glynden..................	1335		
Spartansburg..................	1444		
Summit..................	1634		
Stewart's Switch..................	1460		
A. & G. W. R. R. Crossing CCCLXV	1433		
Corry (*d*)..............CCXV	1420		

a Junction with P. & E. R. R.
b Near Hydetown.
c Union and Titusville R. R. Junction
d Junction with P. & E. R. R.

CCCV. *Pithole Valley R. R.*

Levels on the Pithole Valley R. R. were furnished by Mr. Aug. Mordecai, Assistant Engineer A. & G. W. R. R. at Meadville, Pa.

STATIONS.	Above Oleopolis	+ Lake Erie	Ocean Level.	
Oleopolis........CCCIV	0	446	1019	
Wood's Mills...........				
Prather................	232	678	1251	
Pit hole City..........	290	736	1309	
Pleasantville..........	615	1061	1634	
Enterprise.............	242	688	1261	
Titusville........CCCVI	162	608	1181	

CCCVI. *Dunkirk, Allegheny Valley and Pittsburgh R. R.*

Levels on the Dunkirk, Allegheny Valley and Pittsburgh R. R., were copied from a list furnished by Mr. Henry E. Wrigley, C. E., who obtained the levels from the Engineer in charge of the road.

Datum: Lake Erie.

STATIONS.	+ Lake Erie	Ocean Level.	
Titusville................CCCIV	608	1181	
East Titusville.................			
Pleasant Valley.................	755	1328	
Grand Valley....................			
Star............................	785	1358	
Newton..........................	825	1398	
Summit..........................	878	1451	
Garland.........................	695	1268	
Pittsfield......................	648	1221	
Youngsville.....................	611	1184	
Irvincton.......................	575	1148	
Gravel Pit......................	595	1168	
Jackson.........................	603	1176	
Warren..........................	620	1193	
North Warren....................	643	1216	
Russelburg......................	660	1233	
Ackley's........................	663	1236	
Fentonville (*a*)...............	670	1243	
Frewsburg.......................	688	1261	
A. & G. W. R. R. Crossing CCCLXV	689	1262	
Falconer........................	685	1258	
Ross Mill.......................	689	1262	
Vermont.........................	722	1295	
Sinclairville...................	757	1330	

a State Line of Pennsylvania and New York.

b Surface of water outlet of Chatauqua Lake 675 + Lake Erie 573 = 1248′ Ocean Level.

STATIONS.	+ Lake Erie	Ocean Level.	
Moons	730	1303	
Cassadago (*c*)	736	1309	
Skidmore	744	1317	
Norton's	425	998	
Laona	239	810	
Fredonia	192	765	
Dunkirk (*d*)..CCCLXIII, CLXII	25	598	

c Surface of water 732 + Lake Erie 573 = 1305′ Ocean Level.
d On the list from which the above levels were copied, no elevation was noted at Dunkirk, but as the D. A. V. & P. R. R. and the L. S. & M. S. R. R. use the same depot, the tracks being on the same level, and the elevation as given on profile of L. S. & M. S. R. R. taken as correct, it is therefore adopted as the elevation, at the terminus of this road.

CCCVII. Union and Titusville R. R.

Levels on the Union and Titusville R. R. were furnished through the courtesy of Mr. C. J. Hepburn, Supt. Oil Creek and Allegheny River R. R.
Datum: P. & E. R. R.

STATIONS.	Tide.	Ocean Level.	
O.C.& A.R.R.R.Junc.(*a*).CCCIV	1266		
Hydetown	1239		
Myer's Switch	1230		
Tryonville	1305		
Noble	1285		
Riceville	1356		
Lincolnville	1369		
Lakeville	1399		
Bloomfield	1396		
Union (*b*).....CCXV	1257		

a Junction with Oil Creek and Allegheny River R. R. at Titusville.
b Junction with Phila. and Erie R. R.

CCCVIII. Pennsylvania and Petroleum R. R.

Levels on the Pennsylvania and Petroleum R. R. were furnished by Mr. Aug. Mordecai, Asst. Eng. A. & G. W. R. R., Meadville, Pa.
Datum: Lake Erie.

STATIONS.	+ Lake Erie	Ocean Level.	
Titusville........CCCIV; CCCV	608	1181	
Newton's Mills	685	1258	
Athens Mills	693	1266	
Little Cooley,	630	1203	
Teeple Town	631	1204	
Cambridge	585	1158	
Edinboro	639	1212	
Summit	705	1278	
McKean's Corner	480	1053	
Erie.........CCCLXIV			

NOTE.—The above levels are from the preliminary survey. The road is not yet built, but the proposed line is from Titusville to Erie.

CCCIX. (a) Buffalo, Corry and Pittsburgh R. R.

Levels on the Buffalo, Corry and Pittsburgh R. R. were obtained in Oil City, through kindness of Mr. C. I. Hepburn, Supt. O. C. & A. R. R. R.

STATIONS.	Above Tide.		
Corry Junction..CCXV, CCCIV, CCCLXV..................	1423		
Childs..........................	1474		
State Line......................	1417		
Clymer	1146		
Panama..........................	1545		
Sherman	1568		
Summerdale......................	1629		
Mayville........................	1300		
Prospect........................	1221		
Brockton (*b*).........CCCLXIII	672		

a The levels on this road are supposed to be correct, and may be entirely so, but the profile from which the elevations were copied is indefinite as to the exact location of the stations.

b Junction with L. S. & M. S. R. R. Elevation on L. S. & M. S. R. R. at this point is 724′ above Mean Surface of Atlantic Ocean.

VIII. OHIO LINE SERIES.

CCCL. Pittsburgh, Cincinnati and St. Louis R. R.

Levels of the Pittsburgh, Cincinnati & St. Louis Railroad, were copied from profile in the office of the Company at Pittsburgh, Pa. The profile was furnished by Mr. S. M. Felton, Jr., Gen'l Supt.

Datum: Pennsylvania R. R. levels? Add 7′ for Ocean level.

STATIONS.	Mean Tide.	Ocean Level.	
Pittsburgh (*a*)..................I	(738)	(745)	
Birmingham (*b*)................	760	767	
Jones' Ferry....................	757	764	
Temperanceville.................	762	769	
Sheridan	864	871	
Cork Run........................	874	881	
Ingram	880	887	
Broadhead.......................	872	879	
Cemetery Crossing...............	867	874	
Bridge, No. 3...................	824	831	
Bridge, No. 4...................	787	794	
Bridge, No. 5...................	775	782	
Mansfield (*c*)............CCCLI	775	782	
Walker's Mill...................	820	827	
Oakdale.........................	908	915	
Noblestown......................	923	930	
Willow Grove....................	988	995	

STATIONS.	Mean Tide.	Ocean Level.	
McDonald's	991	998	
Primrose	1023	1030	
Bulger	1146	1153	
Bridge, No. 17	1222	1229	
Burgettstown	1001	1008	
Dinsmore	1082	1089	
Bridge, No. 19	875	882	
Paris Road	858	865	
Bridge, No. 22	829	836	
Collier's (*d*)	826	833	
Holliday Cove			
Edgington (*e*)			
Steubenville (*f*) CCCLV			

a Pittsburgh Union Depot (746′, Gardner.)
b South side of Ohio River.
c Junction with Chartier's R. R.
d In Virginia.
e East side of Ohio River.
f West side of Ohio River and junction with Cleveland and Pittsburgh River Division R. R.

The levels of this road through Ohio are given on page 670, Vol. 1, Ohio Gelogical Survey, 1873; beginning with Steubenville, Washington Street = 155′.

CCCLI. Chartiers R. R.

Elevations on the Chartier's Branch R. R., were furnished by Mr. N. I. Becker, Chief Engineer, P. C. & St. L. Railway, Columbus, Ohio.

Add 7′ to reduce to Ocean level, and substract 1′ for the discrepancy at Mansfield, = 6′.

STATIONS.	Mean Tide.	Ocean Level.	
Mansfield (*a*)....CCCL	776	782	
Leasdale	802	808	
Woodville	807	813	
Bridgeville	825	831	
Boyce's	868	874	
Hill's	873	879	
Greer's	896	902	
Van Emman's	925	931	
Cannonsburg	936	942	
Houston's	952	958	
Ewing's Mills	981	987	
Cook's	1006	1012	
Washington	1049	1055	

a Junction with Pittsburgh, Cincinnati and St. Louis R. R. In table CCCLXXII 775′.

CCCLII. *Hempfield R. R.*

Elevations on the Hempfield Railway, were furnished by Mr. W. N. Bolling, Engineer B. & O. R. R.

Datum: Mean tide at Baltimore, Md., equal Ocean level. (No connection can be made at Washington between the Hempfield and Chartier's R. R. lines.)

STATIONS.	Mean Tide.	Ocean Level.	
Washington (*a*).......... CCCLI	(1049)	(1055)	
Thompson's Mills..............	699	699	
Chartier..........................			
Taylorsville	1008	1008	
Claysville	683 (?)	683(?)	
Vienna...........................			
West Alexandria................	1099	1099	
Valley Grove....................			
Point Mills......................	896	896	
Roney's Point			
Triadelphia......................	734	734	
Elm Grove.......................	683	683	
Carbon			
Mt. De Chantel.................	674	674	
Wheeling (*b*)....................	644	644	

a Continuation of the Chartier's R. R.
b North and Water Streets 644′. Market Place 662′.

CCCLIII. *Pittsburgh, Fort Wayne and Chicago R. R.*

Levels of Pittsburgh, Fort Wayne and Chicago R. R., were copied from the profile (in the office at Pittsburgh), furnished through the kindness of Mr. F. S. Slataper, Chief Engineer.

Datum: Lake Erie. Accepted level of Lake Erie above Ocean level is 573′.

The third column adds 1′ to reduce the levels of the second columns to harmony with those of the Pennsylvania R. R.

It is thus seen that the Depot at Pittsburgh is established from the Atlantic side and from the Lake Erie side, with a probable error of about one foot.

STATIONS.	+ Lake Erie	Ocean Level.	Ocean Level.
Pittsburgh (*a*) I	173.10	746	745
Allegheny........................	165.82	739	738
Outer Depot......................	191.85	765	764
Wood's Run......................	158.65	732	731
Jack's Run........................	156.50	729	728
Bellevue..........................	156.50	729	728
Emsworth........................	153.04	726	725
Dixmont..........................	149.77	723	722
Glendale	149.30	722	721

a Pittsburgh Union Depot.

STATIONS.	+Lake Erie	Ocean Level.	Ocean Level.
Haysville	149.30	722	721
Sewickley	164.30	737	736
Edgeworth	152.80	726	725
Leetsdale	143.44	716	715
Fair Oaks	143.44	716	715
Economy	143.44	716	715
Economy Switch	143.44	716	715
Baden	138.24	711	710
Remington	138.24	711	710
Freedom	130.94	704	703
Rochester (*b*)............CCCLV	134.24	707	706
New Brighton	178.12	751	750
Beaver Falls	198.83	772	771
Sullivan	293.15	866	865
Wallace Run	322.84	896	895
Homewood (*c*)..........CCCLIX	376.76	950	949
Highland	471.28	1044	1043
Summit Cut	481.71	1055	1054
Darlington	408.85	982	981
New Gallilee	385.29	958	957
Enon (*d*)..................434	421.61	995	994
State Line..................472			
Palestine 455	422.46	995	994
Leslie's Run................479			
New Waterford...............503			
Bull Creek..................515½			
Columbiana................555			
Mill Creek 534			
Beaver Creek 487½			
Green Creek.................461			
Gr. Cr. Siding..............454			
Middle York 461			
Franklin..................506			

b Junction with Cleveland and Pittsburgh.
c New Castle Branch R. R.
d From here on the figures on page of the Geol. Survey of Ohio, Vol. I, 1873. Between Columbiana and Franklin is a station now called Leetonia where the New Lisbon R. R. joins. Neither name nor elevation of this point is given, and therefore no connection can be made with Warren by this line.

CCCLIV. Ohio River Water Levels.

Elevation of points above tide from report of Col. W. Milnor Roberts to Canal Commissioners, November, 1840.

	+Lake Erie	Ocean Level.	
Ohio River at Beaver	93	666	
New Castle Pool	222	795	
Conneaut Lake	509.50	1082.50	
Franklin (*a*)	381.50	954.50	
Allegheny River at Pittsburgh (*b*)	120.50	693.50	

a This datum is especially valuable in the final determination of the absolute level of the Allegheny Valley R. R. system centering here. But the

CCCLV. Cleveland and Pittsburgh R. R.

Levels of the Cleveland and Pittsburgh R. R., were copied from profile in office of Mr. Isaiah Linton, Chief Engineer, Ravenna, Ohio.
Datum: Lake Erie; 573′ above Ocean level.

STATIONS.		Above Lake Erie.	Above Tide.	
Rochester (*a*)..CCCLIII		137	710	
Beaver (*b*)	138	137	710	
Industry...............	125	128	701	
Smith's Ferry..........	125	126	699	
Ohio State Line		133	706	
Liverpool..............	120	120	693	
Wellsville	115	115	688	
Linton.................	121	121	694	
Hammondsville	115	115	688	
Salineville	306	306	879	
Yellow Creek (as below)				
Yellow Creek Summit..	543		1116	
Sandy Summit..........	612		1185	
Bayard.............. .	503		1076	
Mahoning Summit......	627		1200	
Alliance	516		1086	
Beech Creek (water)....	446		1019	
Beech Creek (rail)......	471		1044	
Lima.................	525		1098	
Atwater...............	560		1133	
Summit in Atwater.....	603		1176	
Rootstown	550		1123	
Ravenna Public Square..	560		1133	
Ravenna Station........	530		1103	
P. &. O. Canal	495		1068	
P. & O. Canal, rail on bridge	509		1082	
Cuyahoga River water..	456		1023	
Cuyahoga River bridge..	474		1047	
Hudson Village........	547		1120	
Hudson Station.........	480		1053	
Macedonia..............	420		993	
Tinker's Creek, (below rail)................	120		693	
Tinker's Creek.........	248		821	
Bedford................	368		941	
Mill Creek............	210		783	
Newburg	224		797	
Cleveland Euclid street avenue	95		668	
Cleveland Machine shop	56		629	

a Junction with Pitts. Ft. W. & Chicago R. R. 137, (710) is at 350 feet from east end of Bridge. At Rochester Station of that road the elevation is 707.24.
b At Beaver commences a series of levels taken from page 669 of Vol. I, Ohio Geology, 1873.

---

height of the R. R. track about Allegheny River water at Franklin has not been obtained.
b Mr. Gardner quotes from report of City Engineer, March 15, 1871, (page 655, Hayden's Report of 1873), for Pittsburgh:

Low water, City Datum 699.20
High water, 1852................................. 729.88
High water, 1832................................. 732.95

CCCLVI. *River Division C. & P. R. R.*

STATIONS.	+Lake Erie	Ocean Level.	
Yellow Creek (as above) (*a*).....			
McCoy's..........................	111	684	
Elliotsville.....................			
Sloan's..........................	125	698	
Jeddo............................			
Brown's..........................			
Steubenville (*b*)...........CCCL	90	663	
Mingo Junction...................			
Lagrange.........................			
Rush Run.........................			
Portland.........................	90	663	
Yorkville........................			
Deep Run.........................			
Martin's Ferry...................	86	659	
Bridgeport (*c*)............CCLVI			
Bellaire (*d*)..............CCLVI	82	635	

a Down the west bank of the Ohio.
b Junction with Pittsburgh, Cincinnati and St. Louis.
c Junction with Baltimore and Ohio R. R.
d Junction Central Div. Balt. and Ohio R. R.

CCCLVII. *Beaver Levels.*

Bench Marks in vicinity of Beaver, Pa., furnished by Mr. James Harper, County Surveyor, who received the information from notes of Mr. J. N. Hoag, U. S. Engineer.

Bench Marks.

23 Cross cut on door sill of National Plow *Company's building in Rochester*, west door, river front 690.365

26 N. E. corner French and Quay's fire brick works, main building, opposite *Beaver station* on east end top of rubble masonry. Cut on top of rock with cross beside it 688.946

25 Cut and marked with a cross on a flat stone 40 feet from foot of alluvial bank toward river, and opposite a point 50′ west of west end of platform at *Beaver station* 670.348

The above levels were brought from Pittsburgh from a Bench, whose reference above main tide was given by the City Engineer, as determined by the Pennsylvania R. R. level.

CCCLVIII. *New Castle and Beaver Valley R. R.*

Levels on the New Castle and Beaver Valley R. R., were obtained at Pittsburgh, Pa., through the kindness of Mr. F. S. Slataper, Chief Engineer, P. F. W. & C. R. R. (Late survey).

Datum: Lake Erie, 573′ above Ocean level.

This is part of the Ashtabula, Youngstown and Pittsburgh R. R.

STATIONS.	Lake Erie.	Ocean Level.	
Homewood (*a*).........CCCLIII	376.76	950	
Clinton	326.97	900	
Thompson's.....................	286.53	860	
Wampum.........................	228.44	801	
Newport	239.36	812	
Moravia	233.02	806	
Lawrence Junction (*b*)...........	201.09	774	
Mahonington	216.04	789	
New Castle (*c*)..................	230.29	803	
Covert's Mills	217	790	
Edenburg.......................	229.6	803	
Seymour........................	224.3	797	
Hilltown	225.6	799	
Quakertown.....................	244.2	817	
Lowell	252.8	826	
Nebo	266.5	839	
Struthers.......................	263	836	
Haselton	257.9	831	
Youngstown.....................	264.4	837	
Brier Hill......................			
Girard..........................			
Niles			
Warren			
A. & G. W. R. R. (*d*).. CCCLXV			
Champion......................			
Bristolville			
Oakfield			
Bloomfield......................			
Orwell			
Rock Creek.....................			
Eagleville......................			
Austenburg.....................			
Ashtabula (*e*) CCCLXIII			

a Pittsburgh, Fort Wayne and Chicago R. R.

b Junction with Erie and Pittsburgh R. R. at Lawrence. *R. R. track at this point 40′ above water in river.*

c Junction with New Castle and Youngstown Branch of Pitts. Ft. Wayne and Chicago R. R.

d Atlantic and Great Western R. R.

e Lake Shore and Michigan Southern R. R.

CCCLXVIII. Beaver Coals, &c.

Levels of Coal Basins and other points from report of W. G. Darley, Chief Engineer of New Castle and Franklin R. R., Oct. 7, 1864.

	Above Lake Erie.	Above Ocean Level.	
New Castle....................	220	793	
Brier Hill (Mahoning Valley)....	356	929	
Hottenburgh Lower Vein........	520	1093	
Sandy Lake....................	740	1313	
Sandy Lake, Lower Vein........	540	1113	
Harrisville....................	806	1379	
Gillande Summit................	576	1149	
Franklin	417	990	
Mercer	500	1073	

CCCLIX. New Castle and Franklin R. R.

Levels of the New Castle and Franklin R. R., were copied from a profile of the road furnished by Mr. A. Vandivoort, Supt.

Datum: Lake Erie, 573′ above Ocean level.

STATIONS.	+Lake Erie	Ocean Level.	
New Castle (*a*).......CCCLVIII	220.50	793	
Eastbrook......................	333	906	
Graham's.......................	334	907	
Wilmington.....................	355	928	
Neshanock Falls................	419	992	
Volante........................	462	1035	
Leesburg......................	472	1045	
Nelson	487	1060	
Hope Mills	534	1107	
Mercer (*b*)..............CCCLXI	524	1097	
Turner's.......................	571	1144	
Jackson Centre.................	684	1257	
Garvin	754	1327	
Summit.........................	815	1388	
Coulson........................	704	1277	
Stoneboro (*c*).........CCCLXIII	598	1171	

a Junction with New Castle and Beaver Valley R. R.
b Junction with Shenango and Allegheny R. R.
c Junction with Franklin Division L. S. & M. S. R. R.

CCCLX. Erie and Pittsburgh R. R.

Levels on the Erie and Pittsburgh R. R. were copied from the profile in the office at Erie, through the kindness of Mr. E. N. Beebout, Asst. Engineer.

Datum: Lake Erie. 573′ above Ocean level.

a Junction with New Castle and Youngstown Branch of Pittsburgh, Fort Wayne and Chicago R. R. Table CCCLVIII.
b Crossing of A. & G. W. R. R. See Table CCCLXV.
c Crossing, Franklin Division, L. S. & M. S. R. R. See Table CCCLXII.

STATIONS.	+Lake Erie	Ocean Level.	
New Castle (*a*)........CCCLVIII	236	809	
Harbor Bridge..................	243	816	
Nashua.........................	248	821	
Pulaski........................	253	826	
Middlesex......................	260	833	
Wheatland......................	268	841	
Sharon.........................	280	853	
Sharpsville....................	375	948	
Clarksville....................	321	894	
Transfer.......................	417	990	
A. & G. W. R. R. Crossing (*b*) CCCLXV..................	357	930	
Shenango.......................	368	941	
Greenville.....................	388	961	
Jamestown (*c*).........CCCLXII	406	979	
Kasson's.......................	538	1111	
Espyville......................	515	1088	
Linesville.....................	460	1033	
Summit (*d*)...................	586	1141	
Conneautville..................	493	1066	
Spring.........................	388	961	
Albion.........................	284	857	
Crosses........................	192	765	
Girard (*e*)............CCCLXIII	124	697	
Fairview			
Swansville.....................			
Erie CCCLXIII			

d The elevation given at a point near Summit is 573′ above Lake Erie = 1146′ above Ocean level.

e Junction with L. S. & M. S. R. R. near Girard.

CCCLXI. Shenango and Allegheny R. R.

Levels on the Shenango and Allegheny R. R. were furnished through the kindness of Mr. Aug. Mordecai, Assistant Engineer A. & G. W. Railway, Meadville, Pa.

Datum: Lake Erie. 573′ above Ocean Level.

STATIONS.	+Lake Erie	Ocean Level.	
Harrisville....................	767	1340	
Pinegrove......................	677	1250	
Pardoe.........................	632	1205	
Mercer.........................	535	1108	
Cool Spring....................	554	1127	
Freedonia......................	604	1177	
New Hamburg....................	585	1158	
Shenango.......................	364	937	
Greenville (*a*)..........CCCLX	388	961	

a The Shenango and Allegheny R. R. connects with the Erie & Pittsburgh R. R. at Greenville.

CCCLXII. *Franklin Division, Lake Shore.*

Levels on Franklin Division of Lake Shore and Michigan Southern R. R. were copied from the profile in the office of the Company at Cleveland, Ohio, by permission of Mr. J. D. Hawks, Asst. Engineer.

Datum: Lake Erie. 573′ above Ocean level.

STATIONS.	+ Lake Erie	Ocean Level.	
Oil City, east (*a*)...........CCCI	436.80	1010	
Oil City (*b*)..CCCIV, CCCLXVII	436.80	1010	
Reno (*c*).............CCCLXVII	444.50	1017	
Two Mile Run.................	422.00	995	
Franklin (*d*).........CCCLXVII	444.06	1017	
Midway.........................	423.01	996	
Summit..........................	592.02	1165	
Polk............................	511.07	1084	
Raymilton......................	564.88	1138	
Midway.........................	600.88	1174	
Naples..........................	591.78	1165	
Stoneboro	598.08	1171	
Coal Branch	626.08	1199	
Clark's..........................	591.30	1164	
Hadley's........................	497.09	1070	
Salem...........................	424.51	998	
A. & G. W. R. R. Crossing (*e*) CCCLXV..................	414.10	987	
Midway.........................	510.00	1083	
Jamestown (*f*)..........CCCLX	416.78	990	
Turner's........................	487.37	1060	
Simond's........................	483.72	1057	
Williamsfield....................			
Andover.........................	522.20	1095	
Richmond.......................			
Dorsett..........................	444.78	1018	
Jefferson........................	368.07	941	
Plymouth........................	281.20	854	
Ashtabula (*g*).........CCCLXIII	74.52	648	

a Connects with Allegheny Valley R. R. See Table CCCI.

b Connects with Oil Creek and Allegheny River R. R., see Table CCCIV, and with Franklin Branch of the Atlantic and Great Western R. R. See Table CCCLXVII.

c Connects with Franklin Branch of the Atlantic and Great Western R. R. See Table CCCLXVII.

d Connects with Franklin Branch of the Atlantic and Great Western R. R. See Table CCCLXVII.

e Crossing, Atlantic and Great Western R. R. near Salem. See Table CCCLXV.

f Crossing, Erie and Pittsburgh R. R. See Table CCCLX.

g Junction with Main Line of L. S. & M. S. R. R.

CCCLXIII. *Lake Shore and Michigan Southern R. R.*

The elevations of the Lake Shore and Michigan Southern R. R. were obtained at Cleveland, Ohio, through the kindness of Mr. J. D. Hawks, Assistant Engineer.

Datum: Lake Erie. 573′ above Ocean level.

STATIONS.	+ Lake Erie	Ocean Level.	
Dunkirk (*a*)......CLXII, CCCVI	24.94	598	
Morian's........................	53.15	626	
Brockton (*b*)............CCCVI	151.11	724	
Portland........................	121.24	694	
Westfield.......................	123.66	697	
Ripley Crossing.................	163	736	
Ripley..........................	176.75	750	
State Line......................	212.18	785	
Northeast.......................	231.4	804	
Moorhead's......................	194.6	768	
Harbor Creek....................	157.	730	
Wesleyville.....................	123.55	697	
Erie (*c*).................CCXV	112.5	686	
Swanville.......................	162	735	
Fairview........................	162	735	
Girard (*d*)..............CCCLX	143.72	717	
Springfield.....................	90	663	
Conneaut........................	78	651	
Amboy...........................	107.75	681	
Kingsville......................	98.40	671	
Ashtabula (*e*)...........CCCLX	74.52	648	

a Connects at Dunkirk with Erie R. R., Table CCXII, and with the Dunkirk, Allegheny Valley and Pittsburgh R. R. See Table CCCVI.

b Connects at Brockton with the Buffalo, Corry and Pittsburgh R. R. See Table CCCIX.

c Connects at Erie with Philadelphia and Erie R. R. See Table CCXV.

d Connects at Girard with the Erie and Pittsburgh R. R. See Table CCCLX.

e Franklin Division diverges from the Main Line at Ashtabula. See Table CCCLXII.

CCCLXIV. Erie City Levels.

Elevations of points in the City of Erie, Pa., were furnished by Mr. Irvin Camp, City Engineer.

Datum: Lake Erie. 573′ above Ocean level.

STATIONS.	Above Lake Erie.	Ocean Level.	
Chestnut Street, at Second Street (Lake Bluff)................	70	643	
Chestnut and 26th Street.........	190	763	
Water in Reservoir, City Water Works.....................	235	808	

CCCLXV. Atlantic and Great Western R. R.

The levels on Atlantic and Great Western Railway were copied from a profile of road in the office of the Company at Meadville, Pa.

Datum: Lake Erie. 573' above Ocean level.

STATIONS.	Above Lake Erie.	Ocean Level.	
Salamanca (*a*)............CLXII	811?	1384	
Bucktooth....................	798	1371	
Red House....................	771	1344	
Cold Spring..................	785	1358	
Steamburg....................	831	1404	
Randolph.....................	702	1275	
Waterboro....................	690	1263	
Kennedy......................	676	1249	
Poland.......................	694	1267	
Levant.......................	683	1256	
Jamestown (*b*)...........CCCVI	748	1321	
Ashville.....................	777	1350	
Panama.......................	855	1428	
State Line...................	885	1458	
Freehold.....................	974	1547	
Columbus.....................	864	1437	
Corry (*c*)..CCCIV,CCCV,CCCIX	866	1439	
Concord......................	780	1353	
Union........................	724	1297	
Mill Village.................	630	1203	
Miller's.....................	579	1152	
Cambridge....................	585	1158	
Venango......................	556	1129	
Saegertown...................	534	1107	
Meadville....................	504	1077	
Franklin Junction Branch (*d*) CCCLXVII................	497	1070	
Sutton's.....................	526	1099	
Evansburg....................	707	1280	
Adamsville...................	572	1145	
Sugar Grove..................	449	1022	
Greenville...................	384	957	
Shenango (*e*)...........CCCLXI	371	944	
Transfer (*f*)............CCCLX			
Clarksville..................	412	985	
Crawford's...................	318	891	
Orangeville..................	370	943	
Burghill.....................	483	1056	
Johnson's Summit.............	553	1126	
Baconsburg...................	390	963	
Warren.......................	327	900	
Leavittsburg (*g*)......CCCLXVI	322	895	

a Junction with Erie R. R. See Table CLXII.

b Crossing, Dunkirk, Allegheny and Pittsburgh R. R. See Table CCCVI.

c Junction with O. C. & A. R. R. R.; see Table CCCIV. Philadelphia & Erie R. R., Table CCXV. Buffalo, Corry and Pittsburgh R. R., CCCIX.

d Franklin Branch of A. & G. W. R. R. diverges from Main Line three miles southeast of Meadville. See Table CCCLXVII.

e Junction with Shenango and Allegheny R. R. See Table CCCLXI.

f Crossing, Erie and Pittsburgh R. R. See Table CCCLX.

g Junction with Mahoning Division of A. & G. W. R. R. See Table CCCLXVI.

CCCLXVI. Mahoning Division, A. & G. W. R. R.

STATIONS.	Above Lake Erie.	Ocean Level.	
Colman's (a)	265	838	
State Line	259	832	
Hubbard's	328	881	
Veach Mine	350	923	
Doughten's	384	957	
Thornhill	280 ?	853	
Youngstown	290	863	
Brier Hill	338	911	
Girard	310	883	
Niles (b)	336	909	
Warren (c)	327	900	
Leavittsburg	322	895	
Braceville	340	913	
Windham	372	945	
Garrettsville	455	1028	
Mantua	536	1109	
Aurora	515	1088	
Pond	450	1023	
Solan	457	1030	
Plank Road	469	1042	
Newburg	240	813	
Cleveland	24	597	

a Junction with Main Line, A. & G. W. R. R.

b Junction with Niles and New Lisbon R. R.

c Junction with Main Line, A. & G. W. R. R.

CCCLXVII. Franklin Branch, A. & G. W. R. R.

STATIONS.	Above Lake Erie.	Ocean Level.	
Junction (a)	497	1070	
Shaw's Landing	524	1097	
Cochranton	488	1061	
Evan's Bridge			
Utica	457	1030	
Sugar Creek	430	1003	
Franklin (b)... CCCLXII	399	972	
Reno	441	1014	
Oil City (c)... CCCI, CCCIV	422	995	

a Junction with Main Line A. & G. W. R. R. about three miles southeast of Meadville.

b Connects with the Franklin Division of the L. S. & M. S. R. R. See Table CCCLXII.

c Junction with Allegheny Valley R. R., Table CCCI; and with Oil Creek & Allegheny River R. R. See Table CCCIV.

CCCLXVIII. Sharon Branch, A. & G. W. R. R.

STATIONS.	Above Lake Erie.	Above Tide.	
Junction (*a*)	329	902	
Sharon	285	858	
End of Road	275	848	

a Junction with Main Line, A. & G. W. R. R., near Sharon.

APPENDIX.

Mountain Summit Levels.

Statement of elevations of Summits of dividing grounds of Eastern and Western Waters.

SUMMITS.	Tide.	Ocean Level.	
Nescopeck, N. P. R. R.	1635		
Elk & West Creek, P. & E. R. R.	1677		
Sugar Run Gap	2161		
West of Olean, N. Y. & E. R. R.	1672		
Blair's Gap, Allegheny & Portage Railroad	2339		
Wilson's Gap, B. & O. R. R.	2620		
Sand Patch, P. & C. R. R.	2290		
Clarion, P. & E. R. R.	1979		
Catawissa Extension of Little Schuylkill R. R.	1450		
Elmira, N. Y. & E. R. R.	1419		
Chambersburg & Pittsburgh (*a*).	2547		

Note.—The above levels were copied by Mr. G. W. Leuffer from Mr. Strickland Kneass' memorandum, April 4th, 1866, and are supposed by Mr. Leuffer to be from surveys made by Col. Charles H. Schlatter, in 1838 or 1839.

a Summit between Chambersburg and Pittsburgh, on turnpike.

Clearfield County Levels.

Statement of levels in the Clearfield Region furnished by Mr. E. M. Leuffer, Civil Engineer. Add 3′ for Ocean level.

STATIONS.	Tide.	Ocean Level.	
Tyrone Junction of T. & C. R. R. and Pa. R. R.	892	895	
Vanscoyoc	1402	1405	
Gardner's	1553	1556	
Mt. Pleasant	1759	1762	
Emigh's Gap Summit	2025	2028	
Emigh's Gap Summit, Natural Surface of ground	2036	2039	
Osceola.	1473	1476	
Pool, Osceola Dam	1444	1447	

STATIONS.	Tide.	Ocean Level.
Mouth of Beaver Run...........	1444	1447
" Bear Run.............	1467	1470
" Mountain Branch.....	1485	1488
" Whiteside's Run.......	1488	1491
" Wilson Run...........	1633	1636
Crest of Allegheny Mountain at Middle Summit, 3 Spring Gap and source of Moshannon Cr.	2233	2236
Crest of Allegheny Mountain at Northern Summit, 3 Spring Gap.......................	2278	2281
Crest of Allegheny Mountain, one mile east of Northern Summit, 3 Spring Gap, and highest ground.....................	2611	2614
Crest of Allegheny Mountain in gap between north fork of Sinking Run and Mountain Branch..	2406	2409
Crest of Allegheny Mountain in gap between Laurel Run and tributary of Mountain Branch..	2364	2367
Crest of Allegheny Mountain in gap between Bear Run and Mount Pleasant Run..........	2221	2224
Hale's Coal Bank...............	1638	1641
Davis' Coal Bank on pike, two miles east of Janesville........	1670	1673
Little Muddy Run at pike crossing near Janesville.......... .	1450	1453
Whiteside's Gap in divide between Moshannon & Clearfield waters	1618	1621
Confluence of Big and Little Muddy Runs.....................	1321	1324
Spruce Flat Summit in divide between Beaver Run and Clearfield waters..................	1603.5	1607
Confluence of Big Muddy and Clearfield Creek, near Madeira.	1302	1305
Houtzdale, Level of top of rail of Railroad at Depot............	1492	1495
Franklin Colliery Level of bottom of Coal Vein.................	1526	1529
Surface of water in Clearfield Creek at Glen Hope..........	1319	1322
Surface of water in Big Muddy Run at turnpike crossing, 1½ mile west of Janesville........	1345	1348
Hagerty's cross roads............	1568	1571
Stephen's Summit in Clearfield and Moshannon divide	1722	1725
Sand Spring, source of the Mountain Branch	2428	2431
Moshannon Mines three miles west of Osceola (?)............	1465	1468

Centre County Levels.

Elevations of points on experimental line from Bellefonte to Spring Mills, by Mr. J. L. Sommerville, R. E., Bellefonte and Snow Shoe Railroad.
Add 7′ for Ocean Level.

STATIONS.	Tide.	Ocean Level.	
Crossing Nittany Mountain at Heckley Furnace..............	1867	1874	
Head of Penn's Creek (water) ...	1129	1136	
Spring Mills intersection with L. C. & S. C. R. R..............	1072	1079	
Bellefonte and Lewistown turnpike crossing, Nittany Mountain	1650	1657	

CVII. Lehigh and Susquehanna R. R.

See page 43 above.
The following tables have just been received from Mr. John W. Crellin, A. E., in a letter dated, Mauch Chunk, May 1, 1876.

STATIONS.	Elevations.	Ocean Level.	
Top of rail L. V. Track			
Phillipsburg CXIV	217.4		
Easton CVII	215.1		
Glendon	215.06		
Hopes	219.51		
Freemansburg..................	221.73		
Bethlehem......................	235.54		
Bethlehem Junction	239.35		
Allentown	257.23		
Lower Catasaugu	271.02		
Upper Catasaugu................	283.53		
Lauback's....................	303.82		
Siegfried's Bridge..............	315.03		
Priechler's	343.95		
Lockport	356.42		
Walnut Port.....................	371.43		
Lehigh Gap......................	392.73		
Hazardville.........	416.83		
Bowmansville	435.77		
Parryville.............	443.33		
Weissport.......................	475.50		
Lehighton	493.71		
Mauch Chunk................	532.3		
Coal Port.........................	584.7		
Penn Haven Junction...........	708		
Penn Haven................ ..	723.9		

CIX. Nesquehoning Valley R. R.

See page 44, above.

STATIONS.	Elevations.	Ocean Level.	
Nesquehoning..................	801.116		
Hauto	1005.19		
Hometown	1175.64		
Hawk Switch....................	1221.43		
Pamanend	1287.43		

CXII. Lehigh and Lackawanna R. R.

See page 45, above.

STATIONS.	Elevations.	Ocean Level.	
Bethlehem Junction	239.35		
Shimer's	289.129		
Ritter's........................	298.67		
Brodhead's	313.077		
Steubens'	333.257		
Clyde.........................	362.387		
Bath	422.687		
Chapmansville	575.927		

www.ingramcontent.com/pod-product-compliance
Lightning Source LLC
Chambersburg PA
CBHW022337020726
47500CB00004B/1171

* 9 7 8 3 3 3 7 4 2 7 7 8 8 *